A WITCH FOR MR. CHRISTMAS

WITCHES OF CHRISTMAS GROVE, BOOK 2

DEANNA CHASE

Bayou Moon Press, LLC

www.deannachase.com

Printed in the United States of America

ABOUT THIS BOOK

Welcome to Christmas Grove, where second chances gets a dose of holiday magic.

Ilsa McKenzie has only ever loved one man. But eleven months ago, he walked out of her life, leaving her heartbroken and her life changed forever. After leaving the magical town of Christmas Grove to regroup and get her life in order, Ilsa's back, ready to face her past and start her future with or without him. There's only one question. Will Zach want to be a part of her life or will he run again?

Zach Frost doesn't love easily. He's loved and lost before. All he's ever wanted was to run his Christmas tree farm and start a family. And once Ilsa arrives in town, it seems he's on the verge of making his dreams come true. But his past is complicated and it's about to catch up with him. Can he make peace with his mistakes or will he let history repeat itself and lose his chance with the one woman who can make him feel whole?

CHAPTER ONE

*Z*ach Frost stood frozen in the front yard of his neighbor's house, staring at the sweet face of Ilsa's two-month-old baby.

His baby.

Mia Renee Frost. His heart thumped wildly against his ribcage, and his head buzzed with a million unanswered questions. How could he not know he had a daughter until a few moments ago? Why hadn't anyone told him? Why hadn't Ilsa come to him sooner? Why the hell hadn't he called her back all those months before? He opened his mouth, but then closed it when his daughter let out a cooing sound and stared up at him with bright blue eyes. Her cheeks were pink from the cold, and his heart nearly melted when she lifted her hands in the air toward him as if asking for him.

Zach glanced at Ilsa. "Can I hold her?"

Ilsa hesitated for a moment, but then, even as she tucked her daughter closer to her body, she nodded. Her long dark hair spilled over her pale face as she bent her head to kiss her daughter on the forehead. As Ilsa passed Mia over, she said, "It's time to meet your daddy, sweetheart."

The emotion clogging Zach's throat as he held his daughter for the first time almost choked him. Terror warred with an unfamiliar feeling of warmth in his chest. "Hello, beautiful girl." He held her in the crook of his arm and ran a light finger down her nose. The sweet baby blinked up at him and let out a noise that sounded a lot like a laugh. He glanced up at Ilsa. "Is she always this happy?"

A single tear ran down her face unchecked as she nodded.

Zach had a powerful urge to wrap his free arm around the woman he'd dated for a short time a year ago and pull her in for a hug. To comfort her. But then he remembered that she'd kept the news of his daughter from him for months. He knew he bore some of the responsibility for not calling her back, but it wasn't as if she'd been out of the country. She'd only been sixty miles away in Sacramento. She couldn't take a day to drive up to Christmas Grove to let him know he was going to be a father? Panic took over, and he hugged his daughter to his chest as he stared Ilsa in the eye. "How long are you here?"

She frowned. "What do you mean?"

He waved at his friend's house behind them. "How long are you visiting Holly and Rex?" What he really meant to ask was how long did he have to get to know his daughter before Ilsa took her away from him.

"Oh." She tucked a strand of hair behind her ear and shuffled her feet. He could tell her nerves were getting the better of her, but finally she blew out a breath and said, "I'm... We're... Mia and I are back for good." She glanced around, nodding to their friends who were waiting on the porch while Zach and Ilsa had their moment. "We'll be staying here with Holly and Rex until—"

"You both should stay with me," Zach said. *Where the hell had that come from?* The words had flown out of his mouth without a second thought.

"Um, what?" Ilsa reached out and took Mia back into her arms.

Zach let his little girl go without a word even though it felt like his heart was being ripped right out of his chest. Was it possible he'd fallen in love with her at first sight? All he wanted to do was gather her back up in his arms and hold her until he knew all her sounds, all of her expressions, and every detail of her tiny little face.

He pressed his hand over his breastbone and rubbed the ache, wondering what the hell was happening to him. How was it possible to feel so much in such a short time? But even as he asked himself the question, he shook his head, already knowing the answer. He'd always wanted to be a father, right up until that dream had been ripped away from him in the worst betrayal possible. He shoved the memories out of his mind and forced himself to ask the question he had to ask. "You're sure she's mine?"

Ilsa stared at him, her lips pressed into a thin line.

The stormy look on her face told him she wanted nothing more than to tell him to go to hell. And if he was honest, he probably deserved it. But he had to know.

"Yes, she's yours, Zach. You were the only one I was with. The only possibility. If you don't believe me, you can get a paternity test." She tucked her daughter against her shoulder and turned to walk toward the house.

"Ilsa," he said softly. "Wait."

She stopped in her tracks, but her back was rigid and she didn't turn around.

"I'm sorry. I... I believe you." He closed his eyes and took a deep breath. "I meant it when I said you both should stay with me."

She glanced over her slender shoulder. "I don't think that's a good idea."

"I want to spend time with my daughter," he said, keeping his tone soft. "I can help you with her. Get up in the middle of the night to change diapers or help with feedings."

This time she turned to stare at him, her head tilted to the side, studying him. "Zach, you just found out about her. I think you should take some time to process this, and then we can talk in a few days."

"I don't want to take time," he said stubbornly. "I've already missed two months." And the months before that when he could've been at her doctor appointments and reading baby books with her. Rubbing her feet and her back. All the things he'd watched his brother do when his child was on the way.

Ilsa shook her head. "You don't know what you're saying."

"Yes. I do." There was steel in his voice. He knew exactly what he would be getting himself into. And even though he'd just found out he was a daddy, he wanted it more than she'd ever know.

She sighed. "I need to take Mia inside, and this isn't a decision I can make on the spot. You're going to need to give me some time."

Zach felt as if she'd just ripped his heart right out of his chest but said nothing as she walked up the steps where her friend Holly was waiting for her. Holly gave him a look of sympathy before the pair of them disappeared into the large Victorian. Rex moved off the porch to stand next to Zach. "Are you okay?"

"Not even close," Zach said, shaking his head. The anger he'd been holding back started to bubble up from deep in his gut. Who was Ilsa to tell him *she* needed time? She was the one who'd kept his daughter from him. Zach straightened his shoulders and moved toward the porch stairs.

"Whoa, buddy," Rex said, reaching out and grabbing his arm. "Hold on."

Zach stopped and stared at Rex's hand holding him in place. "You need to let go."

"Oh, is that right?" Rex asked as his clear blue eyes flashed with a challenge. "What are you going to do if I don't? Deck me?"

"Maybe. You probably deserve it for not telling me about my daughter." There was no need to ask if Rex had known about Mia. His fiancée was Ilsa's best friend. There was no way he hadn't known. Pain had settled in Zach's chest from the betrayal of the one person he'd always trusted with all of his secrets. He couldn't imagine keeping something that huge from Rex if the situation were reversed.

Rex blinked and then let go and took a step back. "You might be right. But don't tell me you don't remember me mentioning more than once that you needed to call her. That you'd regret it if you didn't."

The anger that had been seizing Zach's body drained away as he stared at his friend. Rex *had* told him to call her. In fact, he'd all but demanded it and had stormed out when Zach hadn't listened. He closed his eyes briefly and let out a long sigh. His voice was barely audible when he said, "You should've told me."

"It wasn't my place, Zach. You know that." Rex patted his friend on the shoulder as he moved past him to grab Ilsa's bags that were still in the trunk of her car.

Zach followed Rex, and as he grabbed one of her bags, he

said, "I guess I do, but you and I both know I'd have been by her side if someone would've told me."

"Yeah, I'm sure you would've. But did you ever stop to think that maybe she didn't want you there out of obligation?"

"Obligation?" Zach asked stupidly. "Is that what you think I feel when I look at my daughter?"

"No. I know better," Rex said, giving him an exasperated look. "But Ilsa doesn't. You basically ghosted on her, man. Then you wouldn't call her back. And why would a woman like that want to move in with her baby daddy after he ignored her for a year?"

Zach stared at the door where Ilsa had disappeared into the house and let out a groan of frustration. He was an idiot. Ilsa was full of life and plenty of self-confidence. And despite the fact that she'd been a nervous wreck around him when they'd gotten together, he'd already known her to be a strong, self-reliant woman. She wasn't just going to move in with him as if she needed a man to take care of her. That wasn't her style, and having a child wasn't going to change that. "You're right." He turned to Rex. "She's not going to forgive my disappearing act easily, is she?"

"Nope," Rex said with a soft chuckle. "You have work to do if you want to get back into her good graces."

CHAPTER TWO

*I*lsa sat in the armchair in the corner of her room, holding her daughter to her chest. She just needed a moment to settle her rapidly beating heart. Her head ached, and she was near tears from the stress of running into Zach the moment she'd arrived at Holly's house. Couldn't the universe have given her an hour or two before she had to drum up her courage to face him?

"Hey," Holly said as she stepped into the room carrying two red mugs. "Can I offer you some cocoa?"

"Yes. Please. Do you have any Irish Cream to liven it up?" Ilsa asked as she tried to smile, but she knew it was more of a grimace.

"Nope. Fresh out," Holly said, placing the mugs on the nightstand. "But I can send Rex out for it if you're desperate." She reached down and gently took the baby out of Ilsa's arms. "Come to auntie, little one. I haven't had nearly enough Mia time."

Ilsa sighed. "Too bad. Not that I'm drinking yet, but after that encounter, I was willing to make an exception."

"It wasn't that horrible, was it?" Holly asked, her tone sympathetic. "I mean, he didn't lose it on you. In fact, he seemed... I don't know. Happy isn't the word, but... moved, maybe?"

"Moved?" Ilsa scoffed. "More like shocked and presumptuous. Can you believe he immediately wanted me and Mia to move in with him? We haven't spoken for eleven months."

Holly pressed a light kiss to Mia's cheek and then looked back up at Ilsa. "Can you blame him? He's lost a lot of time getting to know her, Ilsa."

"You're taking his side?" Ilsa gasped out, horrified that her best friend was defending the man who'd not only ghosted on her, but also ignored the messages she'd left him saying it was important that they spoke.

"Of course not." Holly placed the baby in the crib set up on the other side of the room and then moved to take Ilsa's hands in her own. "I'm on your side, always. You know that. He was a stupid, selfish jerk. There's no denying that. But it doesn't change the fact that he was in the dark about his daughter, even if it was his fault. I can't help but feel a little sorry for him."

Ilsa crossed her arms over her chest and lifted her chin, feeling defensive even if she did see where her friend was coming from. She couldn't help the self-righteousness still swimming through her veins. It wasn't as if she hadn't tried, dammit. And now she was expected to just forgive him after he'd been an asshat?

She was the one who'd cried for days when she'd found out she was pregnant with the man's child. The man she'd secretly loved for years. Then she'd finally thought they had a chance before he'd run with no explanation. For a while there, she'd truly never wanted to see him again. But then her anger turned to resignation, and she knew that she couldn't let her ego and hurt feelings stand in the way of her daughter knowing her father. No matter what had happened between Ilsa and Zach, Ilsa knew that he was a good man. That he would be good to his daughter. And his reaction upon learning he was a father had confirmed her assessment of him.

"I think I just need a little time to process," Ilsa said, as if she hadn't had months to prepare for their meeting.

"It's a lot, I know," Holly said reassuringly. "But at least it went reasonably well, right? He didn't get mad or turn his back on her. That says a lot about him."

"Yeah. Sure." But what was he going to want from them? She'd already turned her life upside down twice for him. Once when she left town a year ago, and again when she knew it was time to come back. What was he going to do when the news sank in? Demand shared custody? A shudder ran through her at the thought. Ilsa couldn't imagine parting ways with her little one every other week. He wouldn't do that to a newborn, would he? She had no idea, and that was the problem. She'd known Zach most of her life. They'd both grown up in Christmas Grove, but she had no idea what he'd do when faced with such a huge, life-altering issue. All she could do was pray that he'd be reasonable.

Holly glanced at the clock on the wall. "Don't you have a meeting with Mrs. Pottson about that position at Love Potions?"

"Yes." Ilsa glanced at Mia and wondered how she'd deal with leaving her daughter for seven hours a day, five days a week. She'd been the manager of a gift shop that Mrs. Pottson's daughter, Mandy, owned. But Mandy, who'd been out of pocket for a number of years, had returned to run the place herself, leaving Ilsa out of a job before she ran off to Sacramento just after the holidays the year before.

It was just as well. With Mia in the picture, she didn't want to work the hours required of management. If she got the job with Mrs. Pottson, she'd go in early before the store opened to prepare for the day and help with the morning rush before taking off to pick up Mia from daycare. "I don't think I'm ready for this. The idea of Mia going to daycare makes me a little nauseated."

"No mom ever is," Holly said, patting her arm. "But at least she'll only be there for a few hours a day."

Ilsa smiled gratefully at her friend. Holly had graciously offered to take care of Mia in the mornings and then drop her off at daycare on her way to work. It meant Mia would only be in someone else's care for a few hours a day. Honestly, it was a dream situation for Ilsa, and she'd be eternally grateful for her friend's help. "Just as long as you're okay with it. Promise you'll tell me if it gets to be too much? It's not like you signed up to be a mom or a nanny."

"Ilsa McKenzie. You just stop that right now. You know how much I've been looking forward to you and my niece coming home. I can't wait to spoil her with love and kisses and Auntie Holly time."

Holly and Ilsa weren't actually related, but they were as close as sisters. And that was enough for Ilsa. If Holly wanted to refer to Mia as her niece, Ilsa was all for it. "Thank you."

"No need to thank me. If it wasn't for my job at the library, I'd be happy to be her full-time caregiver. You know that." Holly moved over to the crib and stared down at the sleeping child. The longing in her expression was unmistakable.

Ilsa knew her friend wanted a family more than just about anything in the world. Her parents had died when she was young, and Holly had been raised by her grandmother, who'd also passed, leaving Holly without any immediate family. Ilsa and Rex were her family now, and she knew Rex shared her dream of having children. She just didn't know if they'd actually started trying yet. It wasn't something she wanted to ask. Ilsa figured Holly would tell her when she was ready for Ilsa to know. "I know, but I don't want you to feel like I'm taking advantage of you. So please, just let me know if it's too much. Okay?"

Holly smiled at her. "I will. Now, go freshen up for your meeting. I've got things covered here."

Ilsa walked over to her friend, engulfed her in a hug, and then disappeared into the bathroom so she could get ready for her interview.

ILSA TOOK a deep breath and walked into Love Potions, Christmas Grove's famous chocolate shop. The rich scent of dark chocolate filled her senses, making her stomach growl and her mouth water. After having Mia, she'd made a concerted effort to eat as healthy as possible, and chocolate hadn't made much of an appearance in her diet recently.

"Ilsa!" Mrs. Pottson called, her round face brightening with a wide smile. "You made it." She had her dark hair pulled up into a neat bun and her bright blue eyes sparkled with joy. "I don't see that little girl of yours. Don't tell me you didn't bring her along with you."

"Sorry, Mrs. Pottson," Ilsa said, giving the older woman a warm smile. "Her Auntie Holly is getting some much-anticipated one-on-one time with her. I'll bring Mia by soon, though, so you can fuss over her."

"Make sure you do that. You know how much I love the little ones." She slipped out from behind the counter and took Ilsa into her arms, giving her a tight hug. "It's really good to see you, Ilsa. We missed you around here."

Tears stung Ilsa's eyes. She hadn't been gone for years. Just eleven months. But still, her entire life had changed since she'd last been in her hometown. Ilsa blinked back the tears, feeling silly for getting so emotional. "You're too sweet."

"Just being honest." Mrs. Pottson grabbed Ilsa by the hand and tugged her into the back room of the shop. "Chase? I need you to cover the store while Ilsa and I work out the details of her schedule."

A tall, well-built blond man appeared from behind one of the shelves. He was wearing a red Love Potions apron and was holding a clipboard. "I'm on it." He placed the clipboard on a desk and then held his hand out to Ilsa. "I'm Chase Garland, Mary's new chocolatier."

Ilsa met the man's green gaze and smiled up at him as she shook his hand. "Nice to meet you, Chase. You must be relatively new in town."

He nodded and shoved his hands into the pockets of his jeans. "It's been two months, and I have to say, it appears I've found the magical town I was looking for."

Ilsa beamed at him. "It is pretty special. I'm a few months late, but welcome to Christmas Grove."

"Thanks. And welcome home," he said before excusing himself and heading into the front of the store.

"He's handsome," Ilsa said as she watched him go.

Mrs. Pottson chuckled. "He is, and he's a great guy, but he's not for you."

Ilsa raised a questioning eyebrow at the woman. "How do you know?"

"I've made my living peddling love potions for over thirty years, dear. If there is one thing I understand, it's love. And the one you're meant to be with spends his days running a Christmas tree farm."

"Stop." Ilsa shook her head even as hope filled her poor battered heart. But before she let that feeling sink in, she squashed it and mentally berated herself for entertaining the idea that Zach had any place in her life other than as Mia's father. "That ship has sailed."

"We'll see." The shop owner winked at Ilsa. "Now, come into my office so we can get our paperwork done."

Paperwork? Ilsa thought. Mrs. Pottson was acting as if this job was a done deal. They hadn't even discussed what exactly it was she wanted Ilsa to do for her. "Um, that sounds great, but would you mind explaining what my duties would be?"

"Of course." Mrs. Pottson grabbed two rolling chairs that had been sitting against the wall and positioned them in front of the neat desk. She sat in one and waved for Ilsa to sit in the other.

Ilsa took her place and crossed one leg over the other as she waited for the woman to continue.

"I understand you're a water witch, right?" Mrs. Pottson asked.

"Yes. I'm pretty good with simple potions and animating water, but I can't control the weather or anything fantastical like that." Ilsa didn't often use her magic. It was sort of like cooking. She could do it, and the outcomes were often decent, but she'd rather just pick up any potion she wanted rather than make it herself. Though she did enjoy making animated water animals to entertain Mia when she was giving her a bath.

"Excellent. That works out well for the position. I want to add a Chocolate Holiday Cheer potion this year as well as another try at Chill Your Tits Cider. Both are pretty obvious, I'd say. Do you think you can make a mood lifter as well as one that relaxes people?"

"I'm sure I can, though we'd need to try out a few different herbs to see which works best," Ilsa said, leaning forward slightly. She liked that Mrs. Pottson was asking for her input. It made her feel as if her skills were valuable. The herbs would help the potion along, but it would be Ilsa's magic that would activate the potions to really affect people's moods.

"Of course. That goes without saying. Every witch has her own strengths." Mrs. Pottson grinned at her. "In addition to the potions, I want to add animated snowmen to my edible gingerbread houses. And perhaps sweet snowflakes that only melt when they hit your tongue. You know, give my gingerbread houses a special touch."

Ilsa chuckled. "You mean in addition to the edible flying reindeer and flashing Christmas lights?"

"Yes. I think it's about time we updated them to have just a bit more pizazz. What do you say?"

Mrs. Pottson's gingerbread houses were already a magical treat for the senses. If Ilsa wasn't mistaken, more than seventy-five percent of the town ended up ordering one for the season. She didn't think they needed anything at all, but she supposed that was part of the reason Mrs. Pottson's business was always booming. She was always innovating and making sure her customers were delighted by something new. "I'd be honored to be a part of them."

"Perfect." She reached over and grabbed a clipboard from the desk. "Just fill this out with all your pertinent information and then we'll work out a schedule." The store owner rose from her chair and started heading for the door. "And don't forget to bring that baby in here sometime soon. I'm dying for a little Mia time."

"I will," Ilsa said, a grateful smile claiming her lips. "And Mrs. Pottson?"

"Yes, love?"

"Thank you."

"No need to thank me, Ilsa. I'm the one who got lucky today." She winked at her once more and then swept out of the office.

Ilsa was grinning ear to ear as she turned her attention to the new-hire paperwork. After filling in her information, she scanned the page, and when she got to the section about her compensation, she blinked and reread the paragraph three times. Then as words started to sink in, tears stung her eyes again, there was no blinking them back.

Her hourly rate was twenty percent higher than she'd anticipated, and there was a bonus structure based on how many of her potions sold, as well as a profit share for the gingerbread houses. If Ilsa's quick calculations were correct, she could end up making more at Love Potions than she had at her previous manager's position in Sacramento.

Ilsa quickly wiped the tears from her face and walked out into the shop. Without a word, she wrapped her arms around Mrs. Pottson and whispered, "Thank you."

The store owner just chuckled, hugged her back, and said, "You're worth every penny."

CHAPTER THREE

*Z*ach tugged the threadbare couch out of his front door and cursed when he stumbled over an old game console that was lying in the middle of his porch. He'd tossed it out there earlier when he'd decided to clear the game room to make room for a nursery. "Come on, you bastard," he growled, strong-arming the couch to get it to clear the threshold. Spruce, his Labrador retriever, let out a bark and ran around to the back of the house, presumably to get away from his grumpy human.

"Need some help?" Rex asked, his familiar voice full of mirth.

"What does it look like, jackass?" Zach's good humor had vanished the day before, the moment Ilsa had walked back into his life. After spending the evening nursing a couple glasses of Jack Daniels, he'd sat in the dark and contemplated what he should do next. He wasn't much of a drinker, but he figured if there was ever a time for liquid courage, it was after finding out you'd become a father two months ago and no one had told you.

"It looks like you're getting ready to rip your door frame off," Rex said, sounding completely unfazed by Zach's surly mood. "Why don't you let me help you with that before you splinter something."

Zach dropped the end of the couch he'd been holding and stared at his friend. After a moment, he said, "Well? Are you going to help or not?"

Rex chuckled as he shook his head slightly. "You're a real prize today, you know that?" He didn't wait for an answer before he climbed onto the couch and disappeared into the house. It wasn't long before he lifted the other end of the couch and said, "Let's do this."

Bending down, Zach lifted his end and said, "Tilt it to the left. I think that should do the trick."

The pair positioned the couch so that it was easier to maneuver and within moments, they had it out of the house, down the steps, and sitting in the front yard. Zach dropped his end and ran his hand through his thick hair. "That ended up being heavier than I remembered."

Rex snorted. "I'm surprised you remember ever moving it. I can't recall a time when it wasn't in your game room. I just assumed it came with the house."

A laugh rumbled from deep in Zach's chest because his friend wasn't far off. He stared up at his large farmhouse, remembering a time when it had been filled with the entire Frost clan. It had been his grandparent's home, and Zach, his parents, and his older brother had moved in after his grandfather had passed when Zach was only seven years old. They were all gone now, every one of them, including his brother. All that was left were the memories and a bunch of old furniture he hadn't bothered to replace over the years.

"Actually, it did come with the house," Zach said. "It started its tenure in the family room and eventually made its way into the den, which is currently my game room. Pretty sure it was new in the late seventies and has been recovered twice."

"And you decided today is the day to kick it to the curb?" Rex asked, eyeing his friend as he shoved his hands in his pockets and rolled back on his heels.

"Yep. The game room is no more. Gotta make room for the crib." Zach strode back up the porch steps and into the house. He didn't stop to see if Rex would follow. There was no doubt in his mind that Rex wasn't going anywhere until he said whatever he'd come to say.

"That didn't take long. Is the crib already ordered?" Rex asked as he followed Zach to the room that would soon be the nursery.

"No. I figured once the room was cleaned out, I'd go to town and pick one up, along with all the other stuff Mia will need when she's here." Zach grabbed a plastic bin he'd found in the garage and started unloading the bookcase that was filled with old vinyl records and books his parents had collected over the years.

"You want to do something with all those game cartridges?" Rex asked.

"Toss them in a garbage bag," Zach said. "I'm going to ask Holly if I can donate them to the library. Or maybe you two know of a family who can use them." They had tons of kids stopping by their holiday tent to enjoy the magical world they created. Surely someone might be interested in his old games.

"Both are decent ideas," Rex said, nodding. "I'm sure Holly will know which is better."

Zach just nodded. He didn't really care either way. The game room hadn't been used more than a few times in the last five years. He'd been meaning to clean it out and turn the space into an office, but he'd just have to continue to use his kitchen table if he wanted to work from the house. Not that he needed to. He had an office that he shared with Rex on the property already. Sometimes he just liked going over the paperwork early in the morning when everything was quiet before he got sucked into dealing with customers at the Christmas tree farm.

Rex kept to himself as they finished cleaning out the room. When they were done, Rex followed him into his kitchen and finally asked the question Zach knew he'd been holding back since the moment he stepped onto his property. "Have you told Whitney?"

"No, I just found out yesterday," Zach said impatiently. "I'll tell her when I see her... probably."

"Probably?" Rex raised an eyebrow. "Don't you think it's better if you tell her before she hears it from the rumor mill?"

Zach closed his eyes and took a deep breath. His gut tightened, and he forced himself to bite back the urge to tell his friend to get the hell out. Instead he gave Rex a half shrug and said, "You're probably right."

"I am right," Rex said, shaking his head. "We both know that, but you're still not going to call her, are you?"

"Not today. That's something I have to do in person." Zach reached into the refrigerator and grabbed two beers. After popping the caps, he held one out to Rex. "Thanks for the help."

Rex took the beer, but didn't take a sip. Instead, he sat at the end of the table and with one arm draped over the back of the chair, he eyed his friend. "Are you doing all right?"

Zach took a swig of his beer and grimaced when the lager hit his tongue. He hadn't eaten yet that day, and just the hint of alcohol had turned his stomach. Without a word, he poured the beer down the drain and then filled a glass with water.

After downing half of it, he asked Rex, "Do you want to go to town and get a late lunch?"

Rex glanced at the clock on the wall. "Just as long as I'm back by four. I promised Maya I'd cover her shift tonight. I think she said there's a school function with her kid."

"Yeah. We can be back by then." Every year Zach hired temporary workers to help man his Christmas tree farm. This was the first year that Maya Rivers had worked for them, but so far, she'd turned out to be one of their best salespeople... Or maybe it was Casey. Her young daughter was always with her, and her sweet smile combined with her enthusiasm almost always closed the deal. Not that Zach was worried about moving trees. The Frost Farm usually had more business than they could reasonably deal with. It was why he'd gone into partnership with Rex earlier that year. The man had a gift for healthy trees and had already proved his worth more than ten times over in the time they'd worked together.

"I'll drive." Rex strode out of the house with Zach close on his heels, whistling for Spruce. The goofy dog appeared suddenly, jumping on Zach and wagging his tail excitedly as if he hadn't seen his owner in days. Zach scratched behind his ears then put him inside before climbing into Rex's red truck.

They were silent all the way to town. Rex pulled the truck to a stop in front of Mistletoe's. The restaurant was a bistro for lunch with a more upscale farm-to-table menu for dinner. They both climbed out of the truck and walked into the restaurant. It wasn't long before they were seated and studying the menu.

Rex put his menu down and said, "So, are we just not gonna talk for the rest of the day?"

Zach rolled his eyes and placed his menu on top of Rex's. "Not if all you're going to do is badger me about Whitney."

"I already said my piece where she's concerned." Rex rested his elbows on the table. "How about we talk business? Maya said something about offering hot chocolate and spiced cider on the weekends. And then Holly said she'd gladly make Christmas cookies for us. I was thinking we could give the drinks and cookies away and just ask for donations for the annual toy drive. I bet we could get Mrs. Pottson to donate the cider and hot chocolate. And there's no question Holly will donate the cookies. What do you say?"

"Mia has Ilsa's eyes," Zach said, unable to stop himself from talking about his daughter. "But that smile? It's totally my mother's. Don't you think?"

Rex blinked at him, seeming completely caught off guard at the subject change. "She is pretty cute."

"What did you expect from these genes?" Zach smiled at his friend, ready to stop brooding. He could continue to be upset about how everything went down, or he could embrace his new reality and do everything he could to show Ilsa that while he'd been thrown for a loop, he was overjoyed at having a daughter and ready to be a permanent fixture in her life. And the first step was to make sure her best friend's fiancé wasn't reporting that he'd gone off the deep end. While Rex was his friend and Zach knew he wouldn't intentionally throw him under the bus, Ilsa was best friends with Holly and all three of them were living in the same house. If Zach continued to be pissed off, eventually that would come out.

Rex laughed and shook his head. From that moment on, the tension between them was broken, and Zach spent most of the rest of the lunch talking about all the things he was looking forward to showing his daughter. Most of them, like learning to ride a bike, throwing a stick for Spruce, or learning to drive, would come much later, but they had a good time laughing about all the trouble Zach and his daughter could get into.

After Zach and Rex left the restaurant, Zach said, "I think I need to walk for a bit and clear my head. Why don't you head back to the farm? I can catch a ride or a hire one of the carriage drivers to give me a lift." He nodded at one of the carriage drivers who was guiding his magical horseless carriage down main street.

Rex glanced at the carriage and then back at his friend. "Are you sure? I don't want to just leave you here."

"You said you needed to be back so Maya could get to her daughter's school thing, right?"

"Yeah. That's right." Rex nodded and glanced at his phone, checking the time. "Looks like I don't have a choice." He mimed tipping his hat to Zach. "Hope the walk helps. See you tomorrow?"

"Yep." It was Zach's night off at the Christmas tree farm, so no one was counting on him to be there. Still, he usually was around if things got busy. He liked to make a point of being available during the season. This year, however, he had more on his mind than just Christmas trees.

Zach watched Rex drive off and then turned in the other direction, walking along the wide sidewalks of the quaint town he'd loved ever since he was a kid. When the store display at the chocolate shop was filled with a flowing chocolate river and the toy store had animated stuffed animals and cars that drove themselves, it was hard for an eight-year-old not to be dazzled. Today, however, it was the slight chill in the air and the faint scent of peppermint that had him smiling. The thought of raising his daughter in Christmas Grove made his heart swell with happiness. No matter what had happened in the last year, he was grateful that Ilsa had decided to bring Mia home.

Bells chimed when Zach slipped into Cherished Wonders, the town's only specialty baby store. Everything was awash in pastels and there was a sweet scent that reminded him of his mother's spring flower garden.

"Well, hello there, Mr. Frost," Bonnie Welsh said with a bright smile. "It's quite a surprise to see you in here today. Have you come to shop for some Christmas presents?"

"Nope. I need to outfit my spare room as a nursery. Can you help me out?" he asked, shoving his hands in his jacket pockets. "It's been a while since I've done this."

Her eyebrows rose and disappeared under her dark bangs. "Nursery? That's... surprising."

He let out a low chuckle. "I see the rumor mill is a little slow then."

"Clearly." She studied him for a moment and then narrowed her eyes. "Well, are you going to fill me in or make me guess?"

He shrugged and decided it was probably better coming from him anyway. "Ilsa McKenzie and I have a daughter. She's two months old. Her name is Mia."

"Two months old and you're just getting the nursery ready?" she asked, her eyes wide.

That made him shift uncomfortably. If he told her he'd just found out about Mia, there would be a ton of town gossip about Ilsa, and if there was any way to avoid that, he would. "Um, she and Ilsa just moved back to town yesterday. It was sort of last minute, so I didn't have time to prepare." It was mostly the truth, although he had no idea how long Ilsa had been planning to come back to Christmas Grove.

"Oh, I see." A smile bloomed over Bonnie's round face. "Well, in that case, congratulations and let's get started."

As he'd suspected, Bonnie took charge and rattled off a long list of items he'd need and then went into a long dissertation about safety and which cribs, car seats, and strollers had the highest safety ratings. By the time she was done, his head was spinning, and he seriously wondered if he'd made a mistake coming to the store on his own. Surely it would've been better to have Ilsa's input.

Someone cleared their throat behind him and then said, "Looks like you could use some help."

He turned and spotted Lily Paddington, one of Holly's friends. She and Holly had become closer that year while Ilsa had been away, so Zach had gotten to know her better, too. "Lily, thank the Christmas gods you're here. I'm outfitting a nursery, and it appears I'm in way over my head."

Lily glanced at Bonnie and gave her a kind smile. "I think he's a little overwhelmed."

Bonnie flushed. "I may have come on a little strong."

A little? Zach thought but said nothing as Lily jumped into action, immediately picking out a crib and stroller.

"These are the ones we got my little sister last year. She loved them," Lily told him.

"Perfect," Zach said, grateful to have someone who knew what she was doing to make the decisions. "Maybe you two ladies can help me with whatever else I'm going to need?"

Lily's eyes lit up. "I love shopping for baby stuff. I'm happy to."

Zach let out a sigh of relief and followed the pair around the store in a bit of a daze, only giving his input when asked. By the time the two were done, Zach looked at the mound of merchandise piled up near the register and groaned. "Um, I don't have my truck with me. I guess I'm going to have to come back for this stuff... just as soon as I find a ride home."

"Nonsense," Lily said with an unconcerned wave of her hand. "I have my dad's truck. Evan is staying with him for the afternoon. That gives me some time. We'll load it up and I'll take you home."

"Lily," Zach said. "You're a true goddess. Thank you."

"I know," she said with a laugh. "But first, as payment, you need to buy me a Mexican hot cocoa from Love Potions."

"Deal."

She walked over to one of the clothing racks, selected a sleeper that had tiny reindeer antlers on the hood and footies that looked like hooves. After quickly paying, she stepped back and said, "Give the woman your credit card, Zach. Daylight's burning."

"Right." Zach stepped up to the counter and proceeded to spend a sizable portion of his rainy-day savings.

CHAPTER FOUR

Ilsa tucked Mia into the baby carrier and then attached it to the stroller her mother had gotten her. Her daughter blinked up at her, her tiny lips forming a happy smile. Ilsa watched her daughter's facial expressions change and sighed with contentment. Before she'd gotten pregnant, she hadn't been sure she'd been cut out to be a mother. She'd had a vague notion of maybe becoming a mother someday, but it hadn't been a burning desire. Ilsa wasn't like Holly. She hadn't craved a nuclear family of her own.

But now that she had Mia, she couldn't imagine her life without the sweet little girl. Her child had changed her, shown her a level of love she hadn't truly believed existed. Ilsa dropped her chin and kissed her sleepy child on the head.

Click.

Ilsa looked up to see Holly standing in the kitchen doorway, holding her camera phone.

Holly smiled tenderly at Ilsa. "Oh, honey. This picture is

27

everything." There were tears in Holly's eyes as she turned her phone around to show Ilsa the sweet moment.

A lump got caught in Ilsa's throat as she eyed the photo. There was so much love and tenderness in her expression that it made her heart flutter. Ilsa swallowed and said, "We need to print that one."

"I'll be getting this one framed." She quickly sent Ilsa the photo through text before pocketing her phone. "Where are you two headed?"

"Gonna take my girl on a walk." Ilsa tugged on her coat and then fitted a tiny knitted cap on Mia's head. It was later in the afternoon and the temperature was dropping, but it wasn't so cold that they couldn't take a stroll through the trees.

Holly cleared her throat and, in a tentative voice, asked, "Are you going to stop by Zach's?"

Ilsa sucked in a sharp breath. "Holly—"

"I know." Holly put her hands up in the air in a surrender motion and started to back out of the room. "It's not my business. I'll stay out of it."

Frustration welled in Ilsa's gut. But she ignored it. The last thing she wanted between her and Holly was tension. Her friend had opened up her home to Ilsa and Mia when Ilsa had expressed her hesitation to move back into her parent's home. Ilsa loved her parents, but she wasn't on the best terms with her mom at the moment. They didn't exactly see eye-to-eye when it came to Ilsa's life choices.

Holly's support was unimaginable, and Ilsa knew she loved both her and Zach. She just wanted them to work things out. But Ilsa had to do it on her own time. She was still having trouble with the way Zach had just decided what she and Mia should do without even having a discussion about anything.

He hadn't even given himself time to process the news. "I'll work things out with Zach. But let me do it on my own time, okay?"

"Of course." Holly nodded at her and then disappeared into the living room.

Ilsa reached for one of Holly's freshly baked gingerbread cookies, and then walked out the backdoor. The slight chill in the air was welcome and reminded her of the walks she used to take with her father right after the first snow of the season. They were quiet times with her dad when he'd listen to whatever she wanted to talk about, and they were some of her favorite memories from her childhood. It was a tradition she hoped to share with her own daughter through the years.

Holly's home was on the backside of Zach's Christmas tree farm, and while Ilsa would have loved to walk through all those glorious trees, it wasn't in the cards with a baby in a stroller. Instead, she pushed the stroller along the paved street, heading away from the Frost Family Tree Farm.

She'd spent the day getting settled in at Holly's and dreading the moment when Zach would show up. Since she was almost out of her emergency savings, Ilsa needed to start working. So even though Mrs. Pottson had told her she could start the next week, Ilsa had declined and asked to start as soon as possible. Mrs. Pottson agreed, and Ilsa was scheduled to go in the next day at five in the morning. That meant she'd have to leave her precious girl for the first time since Mia had come into her life. It pained her to be away from her child for over seven hours, but there was no choice. At least daycare was only for a few hours. She kept telling herself that, hoping she'd start to feel better about it. So far, it wasn't working. It was too bad, too, because Ilsa was certain the caregivers were excellent, otherwise she wouldn't leave Mia there. But it was still hard to put her child with someone whom Ilsa didn't know well.

Ilsa smiled down at her sleeping daughter as she walked down the private drive that was lined with various Christmas trees as well as one giant Douglas fir that Ilsa had always envisioned belonging in Times Square.

She let her mind wander to what it might be like when Zach truly was in the picture. Would he want partial custody? Just the thought made her stomach ache. It wasn't that she didn't trust him. She did, even though their relationship had gone sideways a lot faster than Ilsa had anticipated. He hadn't been a jerk about anything. He'd just stepped back and told her he couldn't be in a relationship. Zach hadn't told her why, he'd just muttered an apology, given her a kiss on her temple, and then left. It had devastated her at the time, but she couldn't fault him for his honesty.

The image of Zach holding his daughter the day before was lodged in her mind. The wonder on his face hadn't escaped her notice, nor had the tender way he'd hugged her before handing her back to Ilsa. She didn't want to admit it, but it was clear that Zach had fallen in love with Mia the moment he'd laid eyes on her.

The thought made her sigh heavily. What was she doing? He was Mia's father. And she'd already kept them apart for two months. With guilt weighing down on her soul, she turned around, determined to find the man she'd been avoiding all year.

By the time Ilsa found herself rounding the corner to Zach's farmhouse, the sun was going down. She was looking forward to getting out of the cold and warming her hands in the fire she knew he was likely to have roaring in his fireplace.

But the moment she looked up at his porch, she stopped in

her tracks when she spotted him with his arms around a slender woman with wavy blond hair. She had her face buried in his neck, and he appeared to be whispering something in her ear.

Ilsa maneuvered herself and the stroller into the tree line and then immediately regretted it. She should've turned around and hightailed it back to Holly's and was intending to do just that, but when she saw Zach pull back slightly and stare down at the woman, she froze again, terrified that he was going to kiss her. Instead, he held her gaze as he said, "Thank you. I would've been lost today without you."

The woman reached up and cupped his cheek as she smiled. "You would've gotten through it. But I'm glad I was able to help." She lifted up on her tiptoes and gave him a kiss on his cheek.

He stood on his porch and watched her walk to the truck parked in his driveway. Ilsa caught a glimpse of the woman's face when she opened her truck door and the light from the cab washed over her.

Lily? Zach was dating Lily? A flash of pain sluiced through her. Zach had never looked at Ilsa the way he'd just looked at Lily. It was a gut-punch that she hadn't been expecting. The man had hurt her months before. She was over him.

Right?

Of course she was. Then why did she feel like her heart was shredding again?

It was just the new mom hormones. It had to be. Lily's truck roared to life, and Ilsa watched as the truck disappeared down the long driveway.

Once she could no longer see the taillights, Ilsa straightened her shoulders and turned to head back to Holly's place. But just as she slipped from the cover of the trees, Mia woke and let out a loud cry.

Ilsa stopped and tugged her little one out of the carrier, pressing her to her shoulder. "Good afternoon, sweetie pie. Did you have a nice nap?"

Mia continued to cry, and Ilsa let out a sigh. "I know. Waking up is hard. Poor thing."

"Ilsa?" Zach asked from behind her.

Dammit. She shouldn't have been surprised he'd heard them. Mia's cry echoed in the still evening. Noise canceling headphones probably wouldn't have blocked it. "Sorry," she said. "I was just out for a walk, and it appears Mia's had enough."

"I can see that." He nodded to his daughter, who was still whimpering. "Why don't both of you come inside and get out of this cold."

"I should get her back to Holly's. She probably needs a diaper change, and I need to feed her. We can... um, talk later?"

"Are you breastfeeding?" he asked.

Ilsa blinked, completely taken off guard by his question. "Um, what?"

"Are you breastfeeding? Because if you are, you can get her settled inside. I have diapers and everything else we need to get her squared away. I didn't get formula because I didn't know if she's on it or if she was, what kind."

"You have diapers?" she asked, astonished. "Why?"

Zach frowned. "Because I have a two-month-old daughter. Why else would I have diapers? Or were you planning on never letting me see her? Because I have to tell you, Ilsa, if that's your plan, we're going to have some real issues to work out. The only reason I haven't been in her life since day one is because I didn't know about her existence. Since you moved back to Christmas Grove, I assumed that meant you wanted her father in her life. If that was the wrong assumption, tell me now so I can get my lawyer on the phone."

The sharpness of his tone startled her and made Ilsa take a step back, clutching Mia to her chest.

"Dammit, Ilsa," he said, sounding exasperated. "I don't want to fight with you. All I want is the chance to know my daughter. To spend time with her and have an opportunity to form that parental bond."

"I..." Ilsa squeezed her eyes shut and shook her head at herself. Didn't she want Mia to know her father? Of course she did. It's why she'd come over in the first place. Just because he was dating someone else didn't mean that she could take Mia and run. And if he had to date anyone, Lily was a great choice. She was Holly's friend and a wonderful mother. She wanted to scream at herself. Instead, she opened her eyes, soothed Mia, who was still fussy, and walked toward Zach as she said, "Of course you do. I'm sorry, I guess I was just caught off-balance." She let out a nervous chuckle. "I wasn't expecting you to have diapers."

"I like to be prepared," he said softly, and he rested a hand on the small of her back as he steered the stroller toward his house. When they got to the porch, he lifted the stroller and left it by the front door as he invited her in.

The place was exactly as she remembered it. Old wood floors that had been refinished ran throughout the house. The stone fireplace hearth gave the room that mountain-cabin feeling. But her favorite feature was the glassed-in sunroom that was on the north end of the house that overlooked Zach's mother's flower garden. She'd passed on a few years ago, but Zach kept her garden going, and there wasn't a single month in the year that there weren't some sort of flowers blooming. Even when the temperatures dropped, something was showing color. She peeked out and spotted the bright red splash of color from the winterberry shrubs and grinned. Those would come in handing for wreathmaking.

"This way," Zach said, leading her down the hallway. Spruce, his golden Lab, ran toward them, but before the young pup reached them, Zach ordered him to his crate and told him to stay. The dog paused, hesitant, but then did as he was told, his head lowered in disappointment. If it hadn't been for the baby on her shoulder, Ilsa might have felt bad for the poor dog. All he'd wanted was a little attention. But he'd been relegated to his bed because of Mia.

Mia took the opportunity to make her displeasure known and let out a wail. Ilsa winced, but Zach turned back, tickled her cheek, and cooed at her. The wailing stopped as she looked up at him in interest. Holy Christmas. How had he done that? Had he been around babies before? He didn't have any younger siblings, and his older brother had passed on in a freak accident more than five years ago. It didn't seem likely that he had much baby experience. But he'd seemed unfazed as if dealing with a fussy baby was old hat. Maybe he'd just gotten lucky.

"Let me take her." Zach held his hands out, waiting for Ilsa to complete the transfer.

"It's okay. Do you have a changing table?" She glanced around the room that was full of baby merchandise, unopened boxes, and mounds of shopping bags. Her eyes widened. It looked as if he'd bought one of everything from Cherished Wonders.

"It's there." He pointed to the wall behind her. "Let me just get the wipes and diapers. They're here somewhere."

"Um, did you get all this stuff in the last twenty-four hours?" Ilsa asked, unable to hide the shock in her tone.

"Today actually." He reached into a bag and retrieved the items they needed to change Mia. "I wanted to be prepared for..." Zach shrugged. "Prepared to take care of her, whenever that might be."

Ilsa blinked, completely taken aback.

"Here. Let me do it." He gently lifted the fussy baby out of her arms and took her to the changing table.

"Oh, Zach, that's okay. I can—" She stopped abruptly as she watched him deftly undo Mia's onesie and make quick work of the diaper. He'd done this before. That was obvious.

"You can do what now?" He smiled at her over her shoulder.

"Okay, where and when did you learn to do that?" she asked suspiciously. "Because that isn't something you just learned today."

He just laughed as he tossed the dirty diaper into a Magic Genie that was already set up next to the table.

"Zach?"

"Yeah?" He picked Mia up and cradled her to his chest. The pure joy on his face nearly brought Ilsa to her knees. "Ilsa?" he asked after a moment.

"Hmm?" She continued to stare at her perfect daughter and the gorgeous man who'd clearly already fallen head over heels for her.

"You called my name, remember? What did you want to ask me?"

"Huh?" She frowned, then shook her head. "Oh, right. Sorry. I was asking how you learned to care for a baby?"

His lips tightened into a small frown. "I used to help a friend out. That's all."

"You did?" The question came out sounding like disbelief, and when he scowled at her, she winced. "Sorry. I didn't mean it like that. I just never knew that. It took me by surprise."

His expression cleared, and he shrugged one shoulder. "It doesn't matter. Don't worry about it." He snugged Mia, pressed a kiss to her tiny nose, and then whispered something to her that Ilsa couldn't hear. Standing there, watching them, made her heart melt into a puddle of goo. Goddess, he was gorgeous, inside and out. She should've come home sooner.

The baby let out an ear-piercing wail and shook her fist in the air.

"Uh-oh. Someone is indeed hungry." Ilsa walked over to them and held her hands out for her daughter. "You'd better let me feed her."

Zach gently passed Mia back to her and then tilted his head toward the door. "Come on. Let's get you somewhere more comfortable. I ordered a rocking chair, but it won't be in for a few days."

"You did?" When was this man going to stop shocking her?

He laughed as he shook his head, amused. "Of course I did. What nursery doesn't have a rocking chair? Come on, Mama. Our kid needs some sustenance." Zach moved toward the door and jerked his head, indicating she should follow.

Ilsa was so stunned by the turn of events, she had no idea what to say. So she followed him into another bedroom—*his* bedroom. Memories of the last time she'd been there flashed in her head. Her entire body heated as she remembered his hands all over her, his lips brushing over her skin, and the weight of him as he hovered over her when they—

"Have a seat," Zach said, waving to an armchair in the corner.

The memories vanished, and she was transported back to

reality as her daughter grabbed for her breast, clearly out of patience. Ilsa chuckled at her. "Okay, little one. Give me a minute."

Zach moved back toward the door. "Do you need anything? A towel or blanket?"

"Nah. I've got it," she said, easing into the chair.

"Okay. Just give me a shout if you think of anything." Then he stepped out into the hall and closed the door behind him, giving her privacy to breastfeed her child. She glanced around, taking in the big king-size bed, the hand-quilted navy and white snowflake comforter, and the two original paintings hanging on the walls. They were charming scenes of downtown Christmas Grove that his mother had painted. She'd sold her art at their family Christmas tree farm for years, but had only offered a few each season, so they were fairly rare and highly sought-after.

The room felt warm. Comfortable. Like *home.*

Home? What was she thinking? This wasn't ever going to be Ilsa's home. But it would be Mia's. Or at least it would be part time. Ilsa sighed. It was time to let Zach be a part of their lives. How could she look at everything he'd done in the last twenty-four hours and not come to some sort of a compromise?

She stared down at the gorgeous child in her arms. Tears stung her eyes as emotion took over. Her entire life had changed in the last year. Ever since she'd fled Christmas Grove, it had just been her and her baby, the two of them against the world. Sure, she had been staying with family, but that wasn't the same as being back in Christmas Grove where she was close to Holly. She was the person Ilsa was leaning on most. Her parents were also across town, and while she knew they'd do anything for her, with the tension between herself and her mother, that relationship was a little bit strained. And now there was Zach.

After Mia had her fill and had fallen asleep against Ilsa's chest again, Ilsa put herself back together and went to find Zach.

CHAPTER FIVE

*Z*ach paced the kitchen, trying to calm his nerves. Ever since he'd spotted Ilsa standing at the edge of his tree line, all he wanted to do was take her and Mia into his arms and hold them. His heart had started hammering, and an ache had formed in his gut at the thought of how he'd stepped back from their short relationship at the beginning of the year. If he hadn't pushed her away then, where would they be now? If only he hadn't taken that phone call from Whitney that day, he might have been a part of this journey with Ilsa from the beginning. Would they still be together? Would he have let himself fall for Ilsa?

He let out a derisive laugh. *Let himself?* Who was he kidding? He'd fallen for her on that first date when she'd been so nervous that she'd been tongue-tied all night. The sassy, self-confident woman he'd known for years had disappeared before his eyes as she'd bumbled through the evening, and he'd found it charming as hell. But then after he took her to the Christmas ball, he'd gotten that call and everything had changed. He'd had responsibilities and commitments to deal with, and starting something with Ilsa had become out of the question.

But now? Things had changed. He had a daughter. And nothing would keep him from being part of her life... or her mother's.

Footsteps sounded on the wood floors a moment later, and Ilsa appeared with a sleeping baby on her shoulder. Zach grinned at her and waved to the baby carrier he'd set on the breakfast table. "You can put her in that and let her nap while we have some cocoa."

He watched her scan the kitchen, her dark blue eyes landing on the pot on the stove. The cocoa was ready. He'd just left it on low while he waited for her to feed Mia.

"That sounds really lovely." She gave him a tired smile and then situated Mia into the carrier. The child settled in, completely undisturbed.

Zach poured the hot chocolate into mugs, added some mini marshmallows on top, and then grabbed a couple of Christmas cookies from his jar before joining Ilsa at the table.

She stared down at the Christmas tree-shaped cookie and grinned. "Did you decorate these?"

"It wasn't my best work," he said with a half-smile and a shrug as he eyed the green icing that had run off the side and the divots that were left by the hard candy ornaments that had fallen off in the jar. He'd made them earlier in the week when a cookie craving had hit, and he'd been too impatient to wait for them to cool.

Ilsa laughed. "I can give you lessons if you like."

He raised his eyebrows, shocked that she'd offered to spend time with him. "Just let me know when."

Her face flushed pink as she glanced at Mia. "Um, I don't

know. I start my new job tomorrow, so I'm going to be settling into that for a while."

"Job?" he asked, wondering why he hadn't realized she'd be going back to work. She'd been a gift shop manager in town before she'd left last January. "Doing what?"

"I'll be working at Love Potions in the mornings. Potions and stuff. Mostly making stock." She gave him a wry smile. "It's a far cry from management, but I didn't want to be working that many hours. Since I'm living with Holly for a while, my expenses will be manageable. It'll work out."

Zach hated the embarrassed look on her face, as if he was going to judge what kind of job she had. It didn't matter to him in the least. In fact, he admired her putting Mia first over her career goals. He knew she'd wanted to run her own business one day, and managing a store had given her the experience she needed. But that was a lot of time and energy when one had a baby to care for. "I'm sure you'll love working with Mrs. Pottson. And you'll get to use your magic. Seems like a good choice to me."

Her smile turned into a grin. "I'll just have to find a way to stay away from her Chocolate Caramel Dreams. If I let myself, I could eat a handful every day."

He chuckled. "Nothing wrong with that as far as I'm concerned."

"Sure, for you maybe." She made a point of scanning his body. An appreciative look flashed in those dark blue eyes. "You can spare the calories when you're hauling trees around all day. Me? All I do is hold Mia, feed Mia, and change Mia. Besides some walks, exercise hasn't exactly been a high priority."

"You know you're not alone in this anymore, right? I'm right here. Bring Mia to me any time. I'd love to spend time with her while you're taking time for yourself." Zach placed his mug down on the table and reached out to take one of Ilsa's hands. She stiffened at his touch, and he fully expected her to pull away, but he held on, waiting to see what she'd do.

Ilsa raised her eyes to meet his. Their gazes held for a long moment. Her voice was soft when she asked, "What are you doing, Zach?"

"Just trying to offer you support," he said. "I am the father of our child. But even if I wasn't, I'd offer as your friend. And that's what we were before last December, right?"

She scoffed. "We weren't that good of friends."

"No, but I wanted to be." His words were honest. As long as he could remember, he'd liked Ilsa. It was just that he'd been unavailable for so long that he hadn't really let himself date much. And then when he'd finally let his guard down, they'd gotten together. Again, he wondered what would've happened between them if he hadn't pushed her away.

Ilsa stared at him for a minute and then averted her gaze. "Thanks. I appreciate that."

Zach reluctantly let go of her hand. He'd have happily held it for as long as she'd let him, but the intimacy was too soon. They needed to find their footing before they moved in that direction... if they ever did. He cleared his throat and sat back in his chair. "Can we talk about Mia's care?"

Her expression turned defensive as her eyes narrowed and her lips pursed into a thin line. "What about her care? Mia has everything she needs. I don't need you to step in and suddenly start judging my parenting skills. How dare you?" She pushed her chair back abruptly and got to her feet.

"Wait!" Zach wrapped his hand around her wrist, stopping her from leaving. "That's not at all what I was implying. Please, sit back down. I just want to talk about spending time with my daughter. And it would be really good to know who's caring for her while you're at work." He let go of her wrist and ran a frustrated hand through his thick dark hair. "Give me some credit, Ilsa. Why would I assume you're a bad parent? Look at her." He gestured to the sweet, sleeping baby. "She's perfect."

The fight seemed to leave her body, and Ilsa sat back down. "I'm sorry. I just... I guess after the way things ended with us, I might have some trust issues to work through."

Zach sat back in his chair, digesting her words. They'd hit him like a sucker-punch in the gut. And the worst part was that he deserved it. It wasn't as if they'd made any commitments to each other. They'd barely even been seeing each other a month. But when he'd gotten that call, he'd bailed out on her without any explanation. Then when he hadn't returned her calls... Yeah, he could see her point. "You deserve an apology for the way I acted." He swallowed. "I'm sorry, Ilsa. If it's any consolation, what happened didn't have anything to do with you. I was going through something, and I just needed some time to work it out."

Her eyes narrowed, and she crossed her arms over her chest, eyeing him with irritation. "I hate when people say stuff like that. What does that mean 'it didn't have to do with me'? Obviously, it did to a certain extent, otherwise you wouldn't have ignored me so completely. You'd have at least called me back. To cut me out of your life, that was a statement all in itself."

How could he tell her that he'd cut her out because he had to? Because Whitney had called, and he couldn't be with Ilsa while dealing with his ex's drama. His sense of obligation to Whitney had overtaken everything, including his own wants and needs. The truth was, he'd cut Ilsa out of his life because if he hadn't, there would've been no way he could've stayed away from her. "You're right. I was… conflicted. It wasn't fair to you, and I apologize."

"Conflicted about what?" she asked. "Getting serious about someone?"

"Yes." Zach grimaced and knew he had to give her something. He had to help her understand why he'd behaved the way he had. "I was close to asking someone to marry me once. Things went south right before I proposed and ever since then, I guess I just decided I wasn't interested in anything long-term. And when things got so intense with us so fast, I just put on the brakes. That's what I meant when I said it wasn't you that did anything wrong."

Her expression softened, surprising him. Then she gave him a half smile and said, "So, I guess that means you liked me. Otherwise you wouldn't have slammed the door so fast."

He shrugged and then winked at her. Yes, that was true. Rex had called him out once about his feelings for Ilsa. He'd told Zach it was obvious he had a thing for her, and Zach had to admit that his friend was right. He'd been playing with fire when he'd agreed to a date with her. And now look at them. They'd both been burned. "Yeah, I liked you." He glanced at Mia and then back at Ilsa. "Now we have a daughter, and I'd really like to help raise her. I might be an ass when it comes to dating, but I think you know me well enough to know that when it comes to family, I'm all in. I won't abandon my daughter."

Ilsa's smile faded as she bit down on her bottom lip.

He held his breath and waited for her reply.

Time seemed to stand still as she stared at him. Her gaze was intense, as if she was having an internal debate. He said nothing, letting her work out whatever was going on in her mind.

Finally, she let out a breath and said, "You're right. You are all in where family is concerned. I never doubted that." She let out a sardonic chuckle. "It is why I came back after all. I guess after seeing you, it just took me a bit to adjust to the reality that I won't have Mia all to myself anymore." There were tears shining in her eyes, but she didn't let them fall.

Zach reached over and took her hand again, this time squeezing in understanding. "You know I'm not trying to take her away from you, Ilsa. I just want to be a part of this."

"I know." She wiped at her eyes and gave him a tentative smile. "What exactly do you have in mind?"

"Well, for starters, why don't we work out some sort of schedule. What hours are you working at Love Potions?"

"Five to noon. Holly will be taking care of her in the mornings before she goes to work, then dropping her off at daycare until I can pick her up."

He frowned. "Daycare? Why would we take her there when I'm right here? I'll take care of her. No need to send her off with strangers."

She blinked at him, confusion shining in her eyes. "You're not seriously suggesting you'll be her daycare provider, are you?"

"Why not?" He gestured to the large picture window that looked out over the path that led to the main area of his Christmas tree farm. "It's not like I have a boss to answer to."

"No, but you do have a business to run," Ilsa said. "How are you going to do that if you have to take care of a baby?"

"Easy. I'll get one of those baby pack things and she can hang with me when I'm out with the trees. Or she can sleep in the office if she's tired while I'm doing paperwork. And if she needs more of my attention, there's plenty of help to watch the farm. It's really not that big of a deal. Besides, the farm is busier in the afternoons and evenings anyway. Cancel the daycare. Tell Holly I'll come get her in the morning around seven."

Ilsa sat there speechless, then she let out a bark of laughter. "You can't be real."

He gave her a slow grin. "Oh, I think you know exactly just how real I am."

"Stop," she said, flushing. But then she grinned, too. "Just because I gave birth to your child, doesn't mean you're allowed to flirt with me."

"Uh-huh. I'll try to remember that." Then he leaned over, meaning to kiss her cheek, but she turned her head at just the same moment and instead, he ended up kissing her right on the lips. Her eyes widened in surprise as they held still, their lips pressed together.

Zach's heart sped up, and the desire to pull her into his arms was right there, brimming at the surface.

"Zach," she whispered and closed her eyes, surrendering to the kiss. He gave in, cupped her cheek, and kissed her with a reverence he'd never experienced before.

CHAPTER SIX

*T*he quietness of five a.m. wasn't new to Ilsa. She'd gotten quite used to the hour in the past couple of months and relished the silence and the start of a new day. Mia had brought with her joyous new beginnings, and each day was full of discoveries and wonder. Only today she wasn't with Mia. She was at her new job, waiting for Mrs. Pottson to come open the store.

The wind blew, sending a shiver down her spine. Ilsa wrapped her wool coat around herself and pressed closer to the wall of the store.

"Sorry! Sorry!" a woman called as she ran toward Ilsa. She wore a knitted hat on her head and was dressed in all black. It was too dark in the early morning shadows for Ilsa to recognize the woman, but her voice sounded very familiar. She pulled out a set of keys and started to unlock the door. "My car wouldn't start, and I had to catch a ride with my neighbor who works at the Enchanted Bean Stalk."

"It's all right," Ilsa said, just happy that someone was there to let her in. She followed the woman inside. "Sorry about your car. The holidays are an awful time to have to deal with repairs."

"Right?" The woman pulled her cap off, revealing a mass of blond hair.

Ilsa stiffened as she recognized Lily Paddington. Guilt coiled in her gut as she remembered the brief kiss she'd shared with Zach the night before. Was Lily really dating Zach? Had Ilsa kissed her coworker's boyfriend? She wanted to groan but held it in as she said, "Lily... Hi."

Lily grinned at her. "You didn't realize it was me?" She laughed. "Surprise. I'm guessing Mrs. Pottson didn't tell you that I open for her most days."

"No, she did not. I thought you were working for Mr. Fredrick, doing his books and for his online mail-order train business." Mr. Fredrick sold enchanted model trains and shipped all over the world. They let off steam and moved along their tracks with no power source other than Mr. Fredrick's magic.

"I am, but he doesn't really need me full time, so I found this to help with the bills. Evan stays with the neighbor before school and by the time he gets out, I can pick him up. It helps that my hours with Mr. Fredrick are flexible. Although, as you can imagine, this is his busy season too, so I'm more than a little overbooked. It's worth it though. It means Evan can have a good Christmas this year."

Lily and her son Evan were relatively new in town, so Ilsa didn't know her story or why Evan's father wasn't in the picture. But she did know they'd struggled quite a bit the year before, so Ilsa was happy that the other woman was doing better. "That sounds like it works out perfectly for you. Holly is watching my daughter for me in the mornings, too. I don't know how I'd do it without her."

Though, Ilsa did know. Her mother would help if she asked, and of course there was Zach, too. She made a mental note to count her blessings and remember that no matter what was going on in her life that she was blessed to have people around her who truly cared. From what she knew about Lily, the woman had her neighbor and now... Zach?

The memory of the kiss Ilsa shared with Zach the night before burned in her brain again. Ilsa hadn't been expecting it. And she knew that Zach hadn't intended to kiss her on the lips. But then there they were, and all the memories of them being together had flooded back and all thought had vanished from Ilsa's brain. All she'd wanted in that moment was to lose herself in that kiss. Her willpower had evaporated right along with the knowledge that Zach was likely seeing another woman, and she'd given in without weighing the consequences.

The kiss had been stupid. She knew that. Once she pulled away, she'd all but fled his house, leaving him with a hasty goodbye and a thank you for volunteering to care for Mia. The night before, Ilsa had only worried about the implications of her own relationship with Zach and had completely forgotten about Lily. What the hell had she been thinking? The guilt curling in her gut intensified, and she glanced away from the woman, hating that she might have walked right into the middle of something.

Not that Ilsa was the only one to blame. If Zach was dating someone, he sure as hell shouldn't have been kissing another woman. But that was on him. Ilsa could only worry about her own conscience. She did not get into the middle of other people's relationships. It was a personal rule and one she wouldn't forget in the future.

"Holly is so great. You know she also offered to watch Evan

for me if I ever needed her to," Lily said as she moved around the café, turning on lights and lowering chairs from where they were resting upside down on the tables. "Having her help in the mornings isn't convenient since we live on opposite ends of town, but I have taken her up on the offer a few times when I needed to run errands. That woman is going to make a great mother someday."

"She really is," Ilsa agreed, moving to help Lily with the chairs.

"Oh, Ilsa. You don't need to do that. Your job is in the lab working on potions. It's my job to open the shop." She waved a hand toward the door to the back of the store. "Go on now. Get settled in and let me know if you have any trouble finding anything."

Ilsa hesitated. "Are you sure? I don't mind helping for a few minutes."

"I'm positive. I've got this down to a science now." Lily gave Ilsa a warm smile. "Do you want anything to drink? Once I'm set up, I can bring you a latte or hot cocoa or tea. Just say the word and I'll get on it."

"Decaf caramel latte would be great. Extra-large with whipped cream." Ilsa covered her mouth as she yawned. "I'm used to getting up early with Mia, but I'm also used to napping after she's had her breakfast. This might be a challenge for me. Hopefully the sugar will perk me up."

Lily let out a bark of laughter. "Honey, anyone who survives the first two months of motherhood can certainly survive a 5:00 a.m. shift at Love Potions. In fact, I'm willing to bet this will be a welcome break from everything you do in a day."

Four hours later, Ilsa had to admit that Lily's prediction had been right on the money. The morning had flown by while Ilsa worked on the potions Mrs. Pottson had requested. The recipes required a certain amount of precision to get right, as did the spells she used to turn them into something magical rather than just tasty drinks. Combined, the work was challenging enough that she'd never gotten bored. In fact, she was so engrossed in her work, that it took her a moment to realize that Chase was standing at the door that led into the shop, scowling. She probably wouldn't have noticed if he hadn't let out a quiet curse.

"What's going on?" she asked the chocolatier who'd spent his morning in the next room working on Aphrodite Passion Squares.

"Huh?" he glanced over his shoulder at Ilsa and stepped away from the door immediately. "It's nothing." Chase ran a hand over his stubbled jaw before disappearing back to his workstation.

Ilsa took a moment to glance through the glass window and then did a little frowning herself.

Zach was there with Mia settled against his chest, the baby carrier at his feet. He was standing near the Caramel Spirit Pops, and Lily was right in front of him, her hand resting on his bicep as she smiled up at him. The three of them looked like the perfect, beautiful family. It was enough to make her stomach churn.

Irritation rose to the back of Ilsa's throat, nearly choking her. She gritted her teeth and stalked through the door, ready to lay claim to her daughter and the man who was her father.

"Don't forget about that dinner date. Early next week?" Zach asked Lily.

Dinner, Ilsa thought. *Really?* He was asking her out while he was caring for Ilsa's daughter? She knew the thought was irrational, especially since she was already certain the two were dating. But did he have to come into Ilsa's place of business and flaunt his relationship in her face? And after that kiss the day before...

Ilsa cleared her throat. "Zach. What are you doing here?"

He turned from Lily and smiled at her, his dark eyes lighting up as he spotted her. Ordinarily that reaction would've pleased her, but the man had just been asking out another woman. If this was the way he was going to behave, then maybe he shouldn't be an influence in their daughter's life.

She crossed her arms over her chest and waited for him to answer.

Zach frowned. "What's wrong?"

Ilsa glanced at Lily, who was still just a few feet away. There was no way she was having this fight in front of the person she'd started to think of as the 'other woman.' Although technically, wasn't Ilsa the other woman? She shook her head and said, "Nothing. Just wondering why you're here. Do you need me to take Mia?"

"What? No. I've got her. I just stopped by in case you were missing her. I figured it would be hard since it's the first day you two have really been apart."

Dammit. Her heart melted right there in the middle of Love Potions. All of her irritation vanished as he handed Mia to Ilsa. Her daughter let out a squeak and reached for Mia's breast, making her laugh. "Are you hungry, little one?"

Zach chuckled. "Hardly. She just sucked down an entire bottle a half hour ago."

Ilsa had pumped and left him with a supply of breast milk that would get him through the day. "She just wants comfort then." She glanced back down at her daughter and smiled gently. "Sorry, sweetie, but Mommy's at work. You'll just have to wait until this afternoon."

Mia didn't seem to mind. Her hands flailed, but her eyes were bright with happiness. Mia leaned down and kissed her forehead. "You're still the most beautiful girl in the world, you know that, sweetie? Mommy loves you." She tightened her hold on the little girl and then reluctantly handed her back to Zach. "Thank you," she said, meeting his dark gaze. "That was really thoughtful," she added as she wiped a lone tear from her cheek.

"You're welcome." He wrapped one arm around her and gave her a gentle hug. "Anytime. Mia appears to love riding in the car and visiting people. So now I'm thinking I'll take her with me when I do my Christmas shopping. That way I can blame her if the recipients don't like their gifts." He chuckled to himself. "Imagine how Rex will feel when he's giving me crap about the fruitcake I hadn't planned to buy him but had no choice because his niece insisted."

Ilsa rolled her eyes. "Do not use my child to get out of taking responsibility for your questionable gift giving."

He laughed. "Okay. She's a little young yet, but eventually I'll be able to blame her. Just you wait."

She couldn't help the chuckle that escaped from the back of her throat. He was going to make a great dad.

The chimes rang on the door, indicating a customer had arrived. Lily stepped back behind the counter, clearly intending to get back to work. But before she could even say hello, Birdie McKenzie cried, "Ilsa May McKenzie. Why is it that I just heard you've been back in town for three days now, and you didn't even bother to tell me, much less bring my granddaughter over?"

Ilsa winced. "Sorry, Mom." Ilsa knew she should've called Birdie. But she'd been so busy settling in and dealing with the personal angst that came along with telling Zach he had a child that she hadn't had the mental capacity to deal with her mother, too. "I was going to come by this afternoon," she said. That was true enough, wasn't it? Maybe not. It had been a passing thought while she was in the shower that morning, but she'd forgotten all about it the moment she'd stepped out of Holly's guest bathroom.

"Uh-huh," she said, clearly not believing her daughter. The woman who everyone said was just an older version of Ilsa turned her attention to Mia. She kissed the baby, cooed at her, pinched her cheeks, and promised her the world all in the span of about thirty seconds. That was what it was like with Birdie McKenzie. The woman was a whirlwind of energy, which had been great when Ilsa was a kid. Her mom was always up for any adventure that Ilsa could come up with. Now, though, her mother used that endless well of energy to always try to direct Ilsa's life.

Her mother's advice was at least partly to blame for Ilsa's decision not to tell Zach about the baby after he hadn't called her back. Birdie wasn't the type of woman to take any nonsense from a man. It was actually one of the traits Ilsa admired about her most. But she was also rigid, overbearing, and judgmental at times. And that was a lot to take even on a good day.

"Mom, please. I promise I'll bring Mia by this afternoon when I get off work," Ilsa said, hoping her mother would accept the offer and move on.

Instead, Birdie scowled at her, shaking her head. "You know that I have ballet class this afternoon. I can't miss it because we have a recital coming up for the holiday. Can we please just find time on the schedule that works for both of us?"

"I can, but not here," Ilsa said, glancing around at the shop that was now filling with customers. "I need to help Lily with this line." Ilsa didn't know anything about working the shop yet, but that didn't matter. Any excuse to exit the conversation with her mother was a good one.

"Why don't you join me and Mia for breakfast, Birdie," Zach said. "I was just about to head over to the Enchanted Bean Stalk."

Ilsa stared at him, shaking her head, trying to warn him off, but it was too late.

"Well, I'd absolutely love the opportunity to get to know the father of my grandchild better," Birdie said in her sickeningly sweet voice that meant she was feeling anything but sweet.

"Mom—" Ilsa started.

"Don't Mom me," Birdie said, cutting her off. "Mr. Frost invited me to breakfast, and I took him up on it. There's absolutely nothing wrong with that." She sniffed as if she were the upper crust of England instead of the wife of a professional landscaper.

"It's not the breakfast I'm worried about," Ilsa whispered in her ear. "It's the interrogation I know you're dying to conduct."

"Ilsa McKenzie. I'm shocked that you said that to me," she said, her blue eyes cold and disapproving. Birdie McKenzie did not tolerate her kids taking her to task about anything, especially something that hadn't even happened yet. "I am merely interested in getting to know the father of my grandchild. And since he offered, I'm taking him up on it."

Groaning, she glanced at Zach and then whispered, "You're going to regret that invitation. I apologize in advance for anything she says or does that crosses the line."

His eyebrows shot up as he watched the older woman walk out of the shop. "Seriously? She can't be that bad. I've dealt with difficult women before. I'm sure it will be fine."

Ilsa just shook her head. "Don't say I didn't warn you." After kissing Mia on the cheek one more time, Ilsa quickly retreated into the back, leaving Lily to deal with the line herself. And honestly, that was probably the right thing to do, since Ilsa would just get in the way.

CHAPTER SEVEN

*Z*ach sat across from Birdie, watching the woman stare down at her grandchild. It was exactly what he'd envisioned when he'd invited her for breakfast. What he hadn't expected was the lecture on safe sex and the expectation that he and Ilsa needed to get married.

"It's obvious you're infatuated with my daughter, Mr. Frost," she said right before taking a sip of coffee. "I have a caterer I can call and a band on speed dial, or even a wedding coordinator who can do all of that for you. All you need to do is get down on one knee and propose. Because no daughter of mine deserves to be a single mother. Trust me when I say it takes both parents, and not ones that are in different households."

"I don't think that's a good reason to get married, Mrs. McKenzie. Don't you agree it's better when a marriage is based on two people loving each other?"

She waved an unconcerned hand. "I married my Ted because he was a good provider. Love is something you can grow into. Trust me, I did and now Ted and I have a great marriage. You will, too."

Zach scoffed. His own parents had been madly in love. And when he thought of his future wife, he pictured himself always wanting to touch her, laugh with her, make love in a way that was full of emotions and more than just a hot hookup.

But wasn't that what you had with Ilsa before you pushed her away? his traitorous mind asked. He shook off the question and leveled a steely gaze at Ilsa's mother. "It's not your place to tell me or Ilsa how we should handle our relationship. For now, all you need to know is that I'm thrilled to have a daughter, and I fully intend to stay engaged in her life as much as possible, regardless of how Ilsa and I feel about each other.

It was Birdie's turn to scoff. "My daughter is half in love with you already, Mr. Frost. Can't you see it when she looks at you?"

Was Ilsa half in love with him? That didn't seem likely considering her moods when she was around him. With the exception of the kiss they'd shared the night before, she'd vacillated between lukewarm and cold. Those weren't the signs of a woman in love. Lust maybe. Love? No. "What I see is a woman who just had a baby on her own and is grateful that I stepped in to co-parent so that everything isn't resting on her shoulders. That's not love, and frankly, not to be rude, but it's not open to discussion either. I think it's time for a change of subject. I won't be bullied into considering something as sacred as marriage by anyone."

"Oh, don't be so dramatic, Zach," Birdie said, sounding impatient. But then she paused and took a deep breath. When she spoke again, her expression had changed, and she looked almost pensive as if she'd given her next words a lot of thought. "I knew your parents, you know."

"Sure." Of course she had. Christmas Grove was a small town, and everyone knew everyone else.

"I know how family oriented they were. And I'm guessing that kind of upbringing doesn't just go away. I'm aware that I'm butting in where I don't belong, but I'd appreciate it if you'd hear me out."

Zach wanted to sigh, but held it in, even though she'd already pressed all of his buttons by insisting he marry Ilsa, as if Ilsa wasn't a completely autonomous woman who needed some man to take care of her. The very idea made him want to laugh. Ilsa was one of the strongest women he knew. Still, he could listen to what she had to say, especially since she now seemed sincere and not just overbearing. If nothing else, it would give insight into understanding Mia's grandmother. "All right. I'm listening."

"I have a confession to make," she said, giving him a small pensive smile. "When Ilsa told me you were the father and you hadn't called her back when she tried to tell you, I was the one who told her to stop trying."

Zach blinked at her, shocked. "Why?"

"Because no one ignores my daughter. That's why," she said indignantly. "I figured anyone dumb enough to cut her out of their life didn't deserve her. Or the right to hurt her. Like that jerk Kevin did. Good gracious, I wanted to throat punch that man. And then only a month or so later, here you were doing the same thing. What is it you kids call it these days? Ghosting?"

Kevin? Who the hell was Kevin? "I didn't ghost your daughter," he said, his voice tight. "I told her I couldn't see her anymore. There's a difference. Ghosting would've meant I'd just stop calling her without any explanation."

"All right, but you did ignore her calls. Isn't that pretty much the same thing?" Birdie asked, this time looking smug.

"No," he insisted, even as guilt crept into his gut. He should've called her back. There was no question. But he hadn't just ended things by disappearing either.

"Whatever you say." She shrugged, clearly not buying his denial. "Just think about what it will mean to go to sleep every night without tucking your daughter in or being there when she wakes up. Is that how you want to raise her? Seems to me that you're the kind of man who wants to be right there the moment anything significant happens in his child's life."

Zach was starting to hate this conversation. But mostly because she was right. Not about marrying Ilsa. The part about wanting to be there for each moment of Mia's life. He was a family man, and it would kill him to have to be a part-time father. "Listen, Mrs. McKenzie—"

"Call me Birdie," she insisted, reaching over and squeezing his hand.

He stared at the connection until she pulled her hand back, acting as if nothing weird had gone on. "First of all, let me just say that I'm uncomfortable with you pushing marriage on either me or Ilsa. I want to make it clear that it's not a topic that is open to discussion. Understand?"

Her smile fell, and disapproval shone from her blue eyes. But she nodded anyway, appeasing him.

"Good. Now, as to your concerns, it is true that family is important to me. And whatever your concerns are, I will not be disappearing on Ilsa or Mia. I will be a part of their lives. Ghosting isn't a thing I do, unlike, Kevin, was it?" He was fishing, but ever since she'd mention another man that had been in Ilsa's life, the name had been pinging through his brain.

"Yes, Kevin." She sighed. "He's the lawyer that got away. I really thought those two would get married, but..." She shrugged. "Instead, he left and Ilsa found herself with you just weeks later. And now we have Mia." She grinned as she looked at her grandchild. "She is gorgeous, isn't she?"

"Yeah," he said, his voice tight. He glanced at his daughter. Or the child Ilsa had *said* was his daughter. How could he know if she'd been with someone named Kevin just weeks before they'd hooked up? His stomach soured, and he suddenly thought he was going to vomit.

Birdie looked up from the baby and shook her head at him. "I know that look." She waved a fork at him. "It's abject terror." Tsking, she took a bite of the veggie omelet she'd ordered. "And that's why I think you and my daughter need to make a commitment to each other. Otherwise, when she moves onto the next Kevin or Jonathon or Clayton, you'll be the one left in the cold without a Christmas tree farm to show for it."

Zach's entire body vibrated with the need to get up and walk away from the woman. This conversation was out of control. "Did you play matchmaker for all of your children even when they didn't solicit advice?" he asked.

"My son doesn't need my help," she said indignantly. "He's always had a good head on his shoulders. Ilsa, however... She's a good girl but too strong willed for her own good. Sometimes her life needs a little nudge." She gave him a knowing smile as if they were in on some sort of secret. He didn't like it. Zach understood that Birdie thought she was helping, but all she was doing was interfering where she didn't belong. "All I'm saying is that I think you two should give it a shot before it's too late. Or, gods forbid, when Kevin comes to his senses and tries to get her back."

Mia let out a cry, and Zach used the noise to his advantage.

He needed to exit this conversation immediately before he demanded answers that Birdie likely couldn't give. He reached for his daughter and said, "I better get her home. I think she's ready for her nap."

Birdie nodded and fussed over her granddaughter for a few more moments before she let them escape. As soon as Zach was outside, he took a deep breath of the cold air.

The name Kevin kept reverberating through his brain. He looked down at the sweet child in the baby carrier and felt sick all over again. Was she really his?

There'd been another man in Ilsa's life, and she hadn't said a word about him. Not even when he'd explicitly asked. Zach had asked if he was the only possible father to Mia. She'd been upset that he'd even suggested such a thing, but he'd needed to know. When she insisted he was the only one she'd been with, he'd believed her. But what about Birdie's revelation that she'd been dating someone named Kevin? Was that a lie, too? He didn't think so. Why would she lie about that?

Zach quickly clipped Mia into the car seat in the back of his SUV and then collapsed into the driver's seat as all of the feeling fled his body. Why hadn't Ilsa told him about Kevin? For some reason, all he could picture was a faceless light-haired man appearing someday and claiming Mia as his own.

After everything that had gone down with Whitney six years ago, there was no room for taking chances. Zach had to know for certain that Mia was his before he became too invested in her. If he found out later that he wasn't really her father, he'd be devastated. It wasn't a chance he was willing to take. He pulled out his phone, scrolled through his contacts, and made a call. Thirty minutes later, he had all the information he needed to get a paternity test done.

CHAPTER EIGHT

Ilsa's nerves were all over the place as she drove up the lane to the Frost farm. She'd started out irritated that Zach had asked Lily out right in front of her, but then had been touched and more than a little charmed when Zach had brought Mia to see her at work. It had been so thoughtful for him to realize how hard it would be for her to be away from her daughter for the first time since she'd given birth. But then the good feelings had fled when her mother walked in acting as if everything was all about her.

Birdie McKenzie was the type of woman who railroaded just about everyone she ever came into contact with. Her unwavering, strong-willed opinions were enough to drive Ilsa batshit on a regular day. But the circumstances of Mia's birth had been something else entirely. When Ilsa had first told her mother she was pregnant and about Zach's failure to respond to her messages, Birdie had been the one to tell her to stop trying to reach him. Then, a few hours ago, her mother had called with a sudden change of heart and had harassed Ilsa to push for marriage, which, frankly, baffled Ilsa. Her mother was a tried-and-true feminist who'd never seemed worried about Ilsa's marital status before. Why did having a child change that? It wasn't as if Ilsa couldn't support herself and her child. She didn't need a man to take care of her.

After Zach had left Love Potions with her mother, Ilsa had spent the rest of the morning wondering just exactly what her mother was saying to the father of her child. If she had to guess, Ilsa imagined that Birdie probably spent the entire breakfast lecturing him about responsibility. She groaned to herself. Zach was the last person who needed life advice from Birdie McKenzie.

It was early afternoon, and the parking lot of the Frost farm was busier than she'd expected for a weekday. But it was early December, and she supposed people were ready to get their decorating on. Ilsa climbed out of her car, and as she was tucking her keys into her pocket, she watched a young blond-haired boy holding hands with his father as they walked toward the entrance.

"Can we get a giant tree like Brian's family has?" the boy asked his father as he stared up at him with wonder in his eyes.

"I thought we'd get a smaller tree this year," the dad said, sounding like he was forcing himself to be cheerful. "You know, like a Charlie Brown tree? One that needs a little love."

"Oh." The little boy was definitely disappointed.

"I thought you loved that movie?"

The boy shrugged. "I guess. It's just that Brian has that giant tree, and I love the way it lights up their front window at night."

"I like it, too, buddy," the dad said quietly. "But we don't really have that much space, and your nana is really looking forward to helping you decorate your tree Peanuts-style. You don't want to disappoint Nana, do you?"

"No." The little boy let out a heavy sigh but then nodded to himself and asked, "Can we get a pink one? That would be cool."

"We can probably make it pink when we get it home," the dad said. Then he muttered, "If we can afford the flocking supplies." The little boy didn't seem to hear him as he ran toward the tree lot, overjoyed to be picking his tree. Clearly the family was having a shortage of cash, but one wouldn't know it to look at them. They looked just like every other family in Christmas Grove. Ilsa wondered if they had enough for other necessities, but she wasn't sure how to go about asking without offending the man.

After smoothing her dark hair and running some lip gloss over her lips, Ilsa made her way up toward the office where Zach had said he and Mia would be waiting for her.

She smiled and inhaled deeply when she passed a table that was set up with cookies and cider. The sweet scent of apples made her stomach growl. She'd been so engrossed in mastering her creations at Love Potions that she hadn't even stopped to consider eating.

"Here. Take one," a young woman of Hispanic descent said, waving at the plate of cookies. "Holly and her baking students made them. They donated them this morning."

Ilsa grinned. That was just like her friend. "Thanks." She took a bite and sighed with pleasure. "Jeez, this is good. And it's exactly what I needed."

The woman nodded her agreement and asked, "Can I help you with anything?"

Ilsa shook her head. "No, I'm meeting Zach at his office."

She held out her hand. "I'm Ilsa, by the way. The mother of the child Zach has been toting around today."

Recognition dawned in the woman's eyes. "Oh, so you're Mia's mama. My goodness, she's a cute baby."

"Thanks." Ilsa started to move toward the office.

"He's not in there," the woman called after her. "He and Mia are over there, helping a couple of families find a tree."

Ilsa scanned the area Maya was pointing at and spotted Zach and the baby stroller near a line of shorter trees. He was kneeling down, one hand holding on to the stroller while he talked to the young boy she'd spotted earlier in the parking lot. The boy's father stood nearby, nervously shifting from foot to foot. "Thanks," Ilsa said, heading their way.

When she was a few feet away from Zach, she heard him say to the little boy, "Did you know we have a raffle going on?"

"A raffle! Yes! Daddy, can we play?" the kid shouted, making Zach laugh.

"We... maybe next time, buddy. Today we only have enough for the tree." The pained expression on the dad's face nearly broke Ilsa's heart.

"Oh, the raffle doesn't cost more. A scratcher comes with every tree purchase," Zach said, winking at the little boy. He reached into his pocket and pulled out a small stack of what looked like trading cards, only they had the Frost Family Tree Farm logo on them. He held them out to the little boy. "Ready to pick one?"

The kid jumped up and down, clapping his hands together. "Can I, Daddy?"

"Sure, buddy." The dad stood back, patiently waiting with his hands in his pockets.

"This one!" The boy pulled the card farthest to the right.

Zach handed him a quarter so he could scratch off the silver coating.

The kid fumbled with it for a moment until his dad stepped in to help him. Once the coating was removed, the dad stared at the card and then at Zach. "Two thousand dollars? Are you serious?" He held it out to him. "Is this for real? What's the catch?"

Zach glanced at the card, grinned at the dad, and nodded. "Congratulations, man! Looks like you won the grand prize. And no, there's no catch. Just pick out any tree you want and follow me to the office so I can get you your prize."

Ilsa watched as all the tension drained from the man and a giant smile broke out over his face. "Oh, wow, Mr. Frost. You have no idea what this means to us." The man shook Zach's hand with both of his and leaned in, saying, "Rent is due tomorrow, and while I have enough for that, I had no idea how we were going to manage Christmas this year. I lost my job six months ago, and while I did find another one, it's really only enough to cover basics. This... It means a little money in the bank and a real Christmas for my family. Just... thank you!"

"You're welcome," Zach said, grinning at the guy. "It's just the spirit of Christmas."

Ilsa walked up to Zach and put her hand on his arm. "Hey," she said softly as she glanced at her little girl sleeping in the stroller. "I'm just here to pick up Mia."

Zach gave her a warm smile. "She's a great salesperson. I think she's single-handedly responsible for selling a half dozen trees."

Ilsa chuckled. "I bet. What did she do? Scream at them so they'd hurry up and pick one?"

"Nah. She has her daddy's charm. Works every time."

"Right," Ilsa said, laughing.

Zach glanced at the sleeping child and suddenly his smile vanished.

"What is it?" she asked, immediately moving to pick Mia up. The child was so knocked out that she didn't even stir. Ilsa held Mia to her chest and pressed her lips to her forehead. No fever. No crying. Nothing seemed out of sorts at all. She glanced back at Zach. "What's wrong? Why did you frown when you looked at her?"

"Huh?" he asked, furrowing his eyebrows. "No, nothing's wrong. I was just thinking about something."

"What?"

"It's nothing." He gave her a forced smile. "Mia's perfect." Then he turned to the man and the child who were waiting for him. His shoulders relaxed, and whatever seemed to be bothering him melted away. "Follow me and we'll get you squared away."

Ilsa tucked Mia back into the stroller and pushed her child toward the office. She took a seat on a wooden bench that was on the office porch and waited while pushing the stroller gently back and forth, knowing that Mia slept better when she was soothed by motion.

"Hey," Rex said, appearing out of nowhere and taking a seat next to her. "How was your first day at work?"

She smiled at her best friend's fiancé. "Good. Or at least it was until my mother came in, humiliated me, and then took off with Zach so that they could 'get to know each other.'"

"You're kidding?" He groaned and leaned his head back against the wall. "How did she manage to rope him into that?"

"She didn't!" Ilsa exclaimed. "The man lost his mind and offered to take her to breakfast. Now obviously, I can't do anything else until I find out what exactly they talked about."

"Huh," he said, rubbing his chin with his fingers as if he were deep in thought.

"What?"

He shook his head. "Nothing, I guess. It surprises me that he offered is all. Zach isn't one for overbearing mothers."

"Who is?" she asked, giving him a strange look. "And when does he ever have to deal with mothers?"

Rex chuckled. "He doesn't. That's the point."

"You're being very cryptic." Ilsa stared into his pale blue eyes, trying to figure out what was going on in that brain of his.

He held up his hands in a surrender motion. "Don't mind me. I was just thinking about the last time he met a significant other's mother. It was... comical. So I can't wait to hear how this went down."

"I'm not his significant other," Ilsa insisted.

"Sure you are," he said with a knowing smile. "You just don't know it yet."

Ilsa opened her mouth to protest, but he cut her off before she could speak. "Where is the man of the hour anyway?" He glanced around the lot. "Do you see him? We're supposed to be discussing some business right about now."

"He's in his office." She gestured to the building behind them. "One of your customers won the raffle."

"What raffle?" Rex asked, getting to his feet. "Someone started a raffle? We can't do that without legal coming in and setting up the rules." He reached for the doorknob to the office, but before he grabbed it, the door swung open and the kid and his father walked out with Zach right behind them.

"Thank you again, Mr. Frost," the father said, shaking Zach's hand.

The little boy wrapped his arms around Zach's leg and

hugged him. He lifted his head and stared at Zach as he said, "Thank you for the tree, Mr. Frost. Now I can put it in our front window just like my friend does across the street."

"There's no need to thank me. You're the one who drew the card that secured your win." Zach patted the kid on the shoulder and then waved as the father took his son by the hand and led him over to where a couple of the staff were ready to load up his very tall Christmas tree.

"What was that?" Rex asked him.

"What was what?" Zach ran a hand through his hair and grinned at his friend.

"You're at it again, aren't you?" Rex asked with a chuckle. "Total sap. You have no sense of self-preservation, do you? If anyone ever catches onto you, you're gonna get taken for everything you're worth."

"Did what?" Ilsa asked, hating that she was out of the loop.

"Your boy here is playing Mr. Christmas again." Rex shook his head and then patted Zach on the shoulder. "We were supposed to go over some orders. I'll be in the office when you're ready."

"I'll be right there," Zach said and then turned to Ilsa. "How was the rest of your day?"

"Boring compared to yours," she said, chuckling softly. "Mr. Christmas, huh? Does that mean there really isn't any raffle?"

He shrugged one shoulder. "There is when I want there to be."

"Right." She nodded, impressed but not surprised that he'd just randomly helped out a stranger who needed a hand. "Tell me something; how is it that you knew they were struggling? Did he say something or—"

"No, he didn't say anything. And even if he had, that's not how it works. Not for me anyway." He reached out a hand as if

70

he was going to cup her cheek or brush a stray lock of hair out of her eyes, but then he dropped his hand and shoved it in his pocket.

Was that his way of making sure he didn't touch her? Disappointment curled around her heart. What was wrong with her? He'd dumped her. And she suspected that he was dating someone else. But she supposed it was possible that he and Lily were just friends. Lily hadn't talked about him at work much, other than to ask about him and Mia. There hadn't been any lingering looks. Maybe she'd read the situation wrong.

But she'd also been the one who got hurt and then spent way too much time mourning the relationship that hadn't really existed when he told her he couldn't see her anymore. And even though nearly a year had passed, it still stung.

"Tell me about this Mr. Christmas thing," she said. "How does it work exactly? Random? Or is there an interview with invasive personal details before anyone can adopt a tree, giving you access to people's bank account information?"

He snorted. "Hardly. It's more of a feeling. Like I can just tell that they are stressed. Nine out of ten times it comes down to money. So I do what I can."

"Like a fairy godfather or something?" she asked as a warm feeling spread through her chest. Was this guy for real?

"More like a selective Santa. Ever since I was a teenager, I just get a vibe when someone needs help. And thanks to what my parents built here, I've been lucky enough that money isn't really an issue for me or the farm. My gift makes it easy for me to pay it forward. So I do."

Ilsa's mouth hung open as she realized what he was saying. His magical gift was the ability to sense when a person was in need. Everyone else she knew who had that gift hated it. It was an ability that drained them because of how much suffering there was with less and less resources to offer people. But not Zach. He'd found a way to help those in need without making them feel like a charity case. And from the sounds of it, he didn't shy away from helping anyone. "That's..." she started, but then she changed her mind and decided talking was overrated. Instead, she took a step closer to him and then kissed him with everything she had.

CHAPTER NINE

*Z*ach hadn't been expecting Ilsa's lips to land on his, but when they did, he didn't hesitate. He wrapped his arms around her and pulled her in close until her body molded to his. She tasted like a hint of chocolate and strawberries, and her hair smelled of vanilla. She was so familiar in one sense, but when he ran his hands over her body, she had more curves than he remembered, and he nearly let out a groan because he found her new shape even sexier than her old one.

"Zach?" she muttered against his lips.

"Yeah?" he breathed, not taking his eyes off her.

"We can't do this."

"Why?" he stared down at her, his emotions churning out of control.

"I think we have an audience."

He dropped his hands and stepped back immediately as he realized they were still standing on the porch of his office, in full view of all their clients and the people who worked at the farm.

Someone let out a wolf whistle while a few others clapped.

"Well, I guess we now all know how that sweet baby came into existence, don't we?" Holly said, heading straight for them with a smirk on her face. She was dressed up in a red dress with a matching red wool jacket and black knee-high boots. His buddy's girl had her hair in a fancy twist, looking like a million bucks.

"Rex is inside the office," he said.

"Thanks." Turning to Ilsa, she said, "Are you sure you'll be okay tonight? I know you worked early and are probably exhausted. If you want me to stay in—"

"No!" Ilsa shook her head adamantly. "Absolutely not. You've been looking forward to this for ages. Mia and I will be just fine, you know, once I figure out how to make a batch of mac and cheese without burning it."

Holly rolled her eyes. "You never burn mac and cheese."

"Nooooow." Ilsa dragged the word out and rolled her eyes. "But I did the first time I made it. Oh, and also a few days after Mia was born. Pro-tip: never cook after being awake for seventy-two hours straight and trying to push a watermelon out of your hoo-ha. Got it?"

"Got it." Holly nodded sagely. "No cooking after giving birth if I've been up for more than seventy-two hours. Is that right?"

Ilsa let out a bark of laughter. "Something like that."

"Noted." She grinned at both of them and then disappeared into the office.

"I thought you and Rex were supposed to go over some orders," Ilsa said to Zach.

He grimaced. "Dammit. We were. But..." He glanced at the time on his phone and then sent a text. A few seconds later, his phone buzzed with a reply. After texting no less than five more times and getting as many responses, he walked over to the office door, pulled it open, and said, "Just forget about the meeting. We'll go over things in the morning. Now go take your girl out before she decides to dump your butt for someone who appreciates her."

"Fine," Rex said as he tugged Holly back out onto the porch. "But don't blame me if they go with another farm because we were too busy to give them a quote."

"I'll take care of it before I go home tonight," Zach said, playfully pushing his friend along. "Now get out before I throw you out."

Holly grinned at Zach, clearly pleased that he'd intervened and that she no longer had to wait around for her man. She blew him a kiss and laughed when Rex protested that she was flirting with the enemy. By the time they made it to the parking lot, their sides were practically glued together with Rex's arm around her shoulders. Their heads were bent together as they talked, and Zach felt a rush of pure jealousy. It wasn't that he was jealous of Rex, or hell, Holly for that matter. No, he was just jealous of what they had.

Zach couldn't remember a time when he'd ever felt that comfortable with a woman, not even Whitney. He glanced at Ilsa still standing beside him.

She looked up at him curiously. "What's going on in that head of yours?"

He pursed his lips together and shook his head. "Nothing."

"Liar." There wasn't any heat behind the word, so he just brushed it off.

"I was thinking that they are perfect together. That's all." It was a lie. He was wondering what would happen if he asked Ilsa out. Would she say yes? And then what? Would they start dating and end up like Rex and Holly? Or would things go up in flames and leave them both charred, just as it had when he'd tried to make things work with Whitney? He took a step back, trying to put distance between him and Ilsa. If he didn't, he knew he'd reach out for her again. But he couldn't. Not now. He needed time to process. Time to get the results of the paternity test back. Then once he had the results, he could think about the possibility of something more with Ilsa.

"I need to get back to work," Zach said, his voice gruff. Gods, he hoped she interpreted that to mean he was tired instead of turned on just by her mere presence.

"Zach, I need to ask you something," she said.

"Okay, anything." He wanted to touch her, but the look on her face was both trepidatious and hesitant. Whatever she had to say, she was nervous about it.

She bit her bottom lip. "Are you... dating anyone right now?"

"What? No. Why? Did you think I was?" He was genuinely surprised that she asked. Did he seem like the type of person who'd kiss her if he had a girlfriend?

"I thought... oh, never mind. I must've misunderstood." She smiled up at him then quickly turned her head as desire flashed in her deep blue eyes.

He was gratified to know he wasn't the only one who was turned on. Ilsa couldn't hide her desire from him, and it was clear as day that she wanted him just as much as he wanted her.

"I thought you had to go back to work," she said.

"I do." But instead of retreating into his office, he just stood there, unable to break himself away from her gaze.

"You're not moving," she said with a chuckle. "What happened today? Did my mother break you or something?"

He snorted. "Not yet, but she gave it her best shot. It seems your dear old mother thinks you should be married. And the sooner the better as far as she's concerned."

"You're kidding. Did she actually say that? The part about me being married I mean." Ilsa pressed a hand over her heart and steeled herself for whatever her mom had done this time.

"She did," he said. "She seems to think you need a nudge in your relationships, otherwise, you'll end up old and alone. And now that you have a baby, your dating prospects are a little slim."

"What?" she cried, clearly horrified, already reaching for her phone. "That woman is getting a piece of my mind."

Zach laughed as he took her mobile phone out of her hand and deleted the message she'd already frantically typed to her mother. "Wait."

"Why?" she asked. "Give me one good reason."

He could give her about a dozen. All of them different places he wanted to touch her body. The desire to take her back to his farmhouse and relive the passion they'd awakened in each other a year ago was at the front of his mind.

But that reckless month had produced a child. One he still wasn't completely certain was his. The thought made him feel as if a bucket of ice-cold water had been dumped over his head, and just like that, all the desire vanished.

Zach blinked, trying to find his equilibrium. Then he cleared his throat and said, "It was nothing. We had breakfast. She tried to get me to ask you to marry me, and I told her to mind her own business. And that was that."

"You told my mother to mind her own business?" Ilsa said, unable to stifle the laughter bubbling up from the back of her throat.

"Yep. I also told her a few things about you being your own person who doesn't need her to run interference, and that neither of us would consider marriage to anyone unless we were madly in love."

"Madly in love, huh?" she asked. "Have you ever felt that before?"

"I thought I did, but looking back, I'm pretty positive it was just strong like." He gave her a wry smile. "How about you?"

"Once. It didn't end well." She averted her gaze, and it was no surprise to him when it landed on Mia. "I should get her home."

"Yeah, right," Zach said, moving to say goodnight to Mia. The child squirmed and raised her fists in the air, demanding more attention. Zach picked her up, pressed her to his shoulder, and showered her with kisses before handing her back to Ilsa.

Her expression when she looked up at him was reverent. And damn if that look didn't almost bring him straight to his knees. He steeled himself, resigned to what he needed to do, and said, "Have a good evening, Ilsa. I'll see you and Mia tomorrow." Then he walked back into his office, closed the door, and held his breath until she and Mia had left.

CHAPTER TEN

*I*lsa sat on the couch with her feet up and stared into her decaf mocha, wishing she could top it off with Irish Cream. It had been that kind of week.

"Here. This should perk you up." Holly sat next to her and handed over a piece of berry pie with a generous helping of whipped cream on top.

"Thank you." Ilsa took a large bite and sighed at the delicious combo of tart berries and sweet whipped cream. "You're my hero. You know that, right?"

"Someone has to be." Holly winked at her and took a sip of her chai tea.

"Why aren't you out with Rex?" Ilsa asked her. "It's Friday night. Don't you two have plans for dinner or something?"

"We did, but Maya has the flu, leaving Zach short-handed. Friday evenings are really busy at the farm, so Rex is working. It's okay, though, because I've been dying for a girls' night. Since your mom has claimed Mia for the night, we should get dressed up and go out on the town. Take a carriage ride to see all the Christmas lights, or go see that new Christmas rom-com that's playing at the cinema. I think it's called *The Package*, which cracks me up every time I hear it. Doesn't that sound just like a holiday porno?"

Ilsa snickered. "It does. But I fear if I go to a theater that I'll fall asleep within ten minutes of the movie starting."

"Not likely if people start taking their clothes off in the first five minutes," Holly joked.

"I seriously doubt that even clothes flying would keep my interest," Ilsa said with a sigh. She'd been up at four every morning for a week. While she loved her job at Love Potions, she didn't love her alarm yanking her out of dreamland in what she considered the middle of the night. But it did allow her to have most of her day with her daughter, so she was learning to live with it. "How sad is that?"

"Pretty sad, especially since it's been an entire year since you've had any action." Holly grabbed a Christmas cookie off the tray she'd left in the middle of her coffee table.

"Don't remind me." Ilsa rested her head on the cushion of the couch. She was so tired even her eyeballs hurt.

"Speaking of action, are you going to tell me what exactly is going on with you and Zach?" Holly's tone was light and curious as if she hadn't just thrown the conversation right into the middle of a mine field.

Ilsa blinked at her. "Really?"

Holly laughed. "Come on, Ilsa. If you can't talk to me, who can you talk to? And after the way the two of you have been throwing the smolder at each other, it's clear whatever was between you before certainly isn't over."

"You're the worst. You know that, right?" Ilsa stared at the half-eaten pie on her plate, suddenly no longer able to eat. She put the plate on the coffee table next to the cookies and buried her face in her hands.

"Whoa." Holly straightened and placed a light hand on Ilsa's shoulder. "I was mostly teasing, but after this reaction, I think you really do need to tell me what's going on. What happened between you and Zach?"

"Nothing." Ilsa lifted her head and stared into her friend's green eyes. "Absolutely nothing. It's infuriating."

Holly frowned. "So you're saying you *want* something to happen?"

Ilsa squeezed her eyes shut and shook her head. "I don't know." Her eyes blinked open. "Yes? No? Ugh!"

Chuckling, Holly wrapped an arm around her and pulled her into a sideways hug. "I've never seen you like this before."

"It's the mommy hormones." Ilsa sniffled. Normally she'd be mortified by her behavior, but this was Holly. She was the one person whom Ilsa allowed to see all of her crazy. If you couldn't fall apart in front of your best friend, who could you trust with your breakdown?

"I think it's Zach hormones." Holly let go of her friend and twisted to sit sideways on the couch. "Listen, I know things are complicated."

Ilsa snorted. "That's an understatement."

Holly ignored her as she continued. "But the chemistry between the two of you is off the charts. It's obvious to everyone who sees you two together."

"Is it obvious to Lily?" Ilsa asked, hearing the bitterness in her tone. She'd asked Zach if he was dating anyone and he'd said no. But when she'd stopped by Mistletoe's earlier in the week, she'd spotted them at a table with their heads bent together, looking awfully cozy. She was pretty sure they hadn't seen her since she'd all but run out of the restaurant the moment the hostess had handed over her takeout order. The image of them had been floating in her brain all week.

"Lily?" Holly frowned in confusion. "Why are you asking about Lily?"

Ilsa shrugged one shoulder. "I think there's something going on with them."

Holly's eyes widened. "What? When? How?"

"I saw them together last week at his house and then again at Mistletoe's. They looked like they were on a date." Ilsa tried to make it sound like the very idea didn't make her want to vomit, but she was pretty sure Holly saw right through her.

"Honey, if there was something going on with Lily and Zach, I'd know. That dinner you saw them at was just Zach thanking her for helping him get Mia's room put together. Besides, Lily would tell me if it had been more," Holly said, with an air of confidence. "Or Zach would tell Rex. And according to Rex, you and Mia are the only two people Zach has been talking about this week."

Ilsa slumped back against the couch, still unconvinced. "Are you sure? Because I swear, I thought... I saw him hugging her and..." She held her hands up in the air. "It looked like more than friendship."

Holly squeezed her hand. "I'm pretty sure. Don't you think that if they were, there'd be a lot more talk around this town? What a scandal that would be. Zach with a new baby and a new girlfriend who isn't the mother of his child? That is tabloid fodder right there."

Ilsa had to admit that Holly had a point. And it wasn't as if Zach had much time to spend with someone else. Over the past week, the three of them had settled into a rhythm. Zach picked Mia up shortly after seven in the morning. He'd then go by Love Potions and hang around while Ilsa took a break to snuggle with Mia. Then after work, Ilsa came back to Holly's to clean up before heading over to the farm to get Mia in the early afternoon.

Zach was a great caregiver. That was obvious. Mia had taken to him right away, and each day when Ilsa picked her up, she was animated and happy. Ilsa had started to wonder what it would've been like if she'd taken him up on his offer for them to live with him. But when she thought of it, her mind immediately focused on the two different times she was sure he was going to kiss her. He wouldn't have acted like he wanted her if he had a girlfriend, would he? He wasn't that kind of guy.

There was the day at the Christmas tree farm when she'd been sure he wanted to kiss her, and then it almost happened again a few days ago on her break. They'd been laughing about something she didn't even remember, and when she finally caught her breath, he was right there, his eyes sparkling as he stared at her lips. She'd been ready to move in when he jerked back and made an excuse about needing to get back to work. If she'd allowed herself to live with him, would everything be different now? Holly was right; their chemistry was off the charts. She figured they'd have only lasted a few days before they started sleeping in the same bed every night. She groaned, hating that she was so unsure about what she wanted and how she was feeling.

Holly patted her on the knee. "Why don't you just tell him how you feel?"

"Just tell him?" Ilsa asked. "Have you lost your mind? First of all, he dumped me. So if you think I'm going to throw myself at him just because he looks really good in those faded jeans, you've lost your mind. Besides, we have Mia to think about. I can't mess things up with her dad. We need to stay friends so we can raise our daughter together."

"Have you let yourself think about what would happen if you did get together... and *stayed* together?" Holly asked.

Ilsa abruptly got to her feet. "Don't say things like that."

"Why not?" Holly stared up at her with her head tilted to the side.

"Because if I let myself hope for that, it's just playing with fire." Ilsa stormed out of the room, into the kitchen, and kept going right out the back door. Her head was spinning with Holly's suggestion. Was her friend crazy? Insane? Ilsa couldn't just tell Zach she was still into him. What would that accomplish? They'd end up in bed together, and then everything would get awkward. What would that mean for Mia? While Zach was obviously attracted to Ilsa, it was abundantly clear he wasn't interested in taking things further. Otherwise, he'd have taken one of the opportunities to kiss her. It wasn't as if she hadn't made it perfectly clear she was willing. For her daughter's sake, Ilsa couldn't risk putting a wedge between her and Zach.

The cool air chilled her skin. But instead of going back inside, Ilsa sat on the back step and stared up at the bright stars. It was a clear night, one that was cold enough that they might even get a little snow. Her lips curled up in a smile as she imagined Mia a little older, building a snowman in the yard. Only the yard wasn't Holly's in her imagination; it was Zach's.

Irritation crawled up her spine and she silently berated herself for thinking about Zach again. Why was he never far from her thoughts? Why couldn't she get him out of her head?

She knew why. She'd been attracted to him for as long as she could remember, and then when they'd finally gotten together, she'd fallen hook, line, and sinker for him. The man was kind, generous, honest, and to top it all off, the sexiest man she'd ever seen. How could she not fall for him? When he'd told her that he needed to stop seeing her, she'd taken it in stride. Mostly. And even though it wasn't easy, she'd gotten to a place of acceptance. But then she'd realized she was pregnant, and suddenly, there were life decisions that were a lot more important than worrying about whether or not Zach wanted to date her.

The creak of a door opening sounded behind her.

Ilsa stood, finding Holly standing in the doorway, and she asked, "What are you doing?"

"Nothing." Holly held a mug close to her lips as if she were going to take a sip.

"Liar. You were watching me," Ilsa said, her hands on her hips.

Holly rolled her eyes. "Of course I was watching you. When your friend flies out the door looking pissed off like someone had just kicked her puppy, you pay attention, make sure they're okay."

"I'm fine now. Just needed a moment to myself," Ilsa said, waving to the back porch.

"I can see that." Holly took a step forward and held her arms out wide, inviting a hug. Ilsa didn't hesitate. She wrapped her arms around her friend and said, "Will you punch me if I ever act like this again? I can't believe how upset I am over a guy. What am I, thirteen?"

"Punch you?" Holly said with a wry smile. "No. Not happening. But I will be happy to remind you that you're a strong independent woman who doesn't need Zach. Honestly, Ilsa, you two are making this work so well, you're right to be cautious. I'm sorry for teasing you about him."

"I just wish he didn't get under my skin so much," Ilsa said. "It would be so much easier if I just felt nothing when I see him."

"I know." Holly held the door open for her. Ilsa took one last look at the tree line that led to Zach's place, scowled in his direction, and then went back inside so that she and Holly could watch the Hallmark Channel and talk dirt about all their exes. They capped the night off by singing to Taylor Swift's "The Man" at the top of their lungs.

By the time Ilsa's mother appeared with the baby at just past nine, Ilsa had decided that it had been one of the best nights she'd had since before Mia was born.

"You look drunk," Birdie said, eyeing Ilsa as she clutched Mia to her chest.

"Nice try, Mom, but I haven't had anything to drink in months." She gently took her daughter and laid her in the baby carrier where she liked to sleep.

"She's just high on life, Birdie," Holly said, almost choking on her laughter.

Birdie glanced around, shaking her head. "I'm glad you two are having fun now while you can. Pretty soon you'll both be married, and nights like these will be a thing of the past."

Ilsa rolled her eyes and said, "Let's not do this tonight, Mom."

"Do what?" Birdie looked genuinely confused.

"Dismiss important relationships over some hypothetical future situation."

"What?" Birdie's forehead wrinkled. "That wasn't what I was doing. I was just saying that life changes. It's to be expected."

No that wasn't what she was saying. Her mother was implying that marriage sucked some of the joy out of life. She'd always made comments like that, and for whatever reason, Ilsa hadn't really paid them much thought. But now she was wondering if her mother felt like she'd missed out on a lot of what her life could've been if she hadn't married young. Ilsa loved her father. He was a good man, and Ilsa felt confident that he'd never intentionally held Birdie back from anything she wanted to do. "Mom, why do you think life stops after you marry someone?"

"I don't think that." Birdie crossed her arms over her chest and stared at her daughter in defiance. "Why are you asking me that?"

Ilsa waved a hand at Holly. "You just said girls' nights will be a thing of the past once we both get married. Why would that be the case? Holly lives with Rex, and here we are, having a really fun night."

Birdie tsked, looking annoyed. "I just meant that life changes. You have more responsibilities with a husband and kids. That's all." She huffed out a breath. "Why are you always fighting me these days? I'm only trying to help."

Ilsa glanced at her daughter and then back at her mother. She truly believed that Birdie was trying to offer words of wisdom. Ilsa just wished her mother could be more positive sometimes. "I'm sorry, Mom." Ilsa wrapped her mother in a hug. "Thank you for taking care of Mia tonight. It's because of you that I was able to relax with Holly for a few hours. I appreciate it."

Her mother sank into the hug, holding her daughter close. "You know I love that little girl. Any time you're willing to let me take her, you just let me know." She pulled back and looked into her daughter's eyes. "But don't think I'm a built-in babysitter like Gretchen's daughter does. I swear, that girl is dropping her kids off every other day. Why, just Tuesday, Gretchen had to cancel her hair appointment for the second time in a row because Vanessa just had to go down to Sacramento to see her new man. And now Gretchen's roots are showing so badly, she hasn't left the house without a cap in over two weeks. She even wore one to the holiday fundraiser." Birdie shuddered. "That knit cap did not go well with her sparkling red cocktail dress."

Ilsa chuckled. "Don't worry, Mom. I won't ever make you miss a hair appointment. That would be sacrilege."

"You're a good girl, Ilsa." Birdie patted her daughter's arm, moved to the carrier to kiss Mia goodbye, and then left with a smile on her face.

"Good save," Holly said.

Ilsa sighed and flopped back down on the couch. "I do love her, but man. Some days."

"I know." Holly handed her another cookie. "I think it's time for another Hallmark movie."

CHAPTER ELEVEN

*I*lsa had all but decided she'd been wrong about her suspicions of Zach and Lily dating. Other than the night when she saw them outside his house and the one evening when she saw them at dinner, she didn't have any reason to believe that they were anything more than friends.

People were allowed to have friends of the opposite sex. She knew that. Rex was her friend, right? He gave her hugs, and there was absolutely nothing sexual about it. It also wouldn't be out of the realm of possibility that they'd have dinner together if Holly was busy.

It was just too bad that Ilsa had been burned before, and now that distrust was always lurking. That, more than anything, was why she hated Kevin so much. Her ex had cheated on her not once, but twice. They hadn't ever been serious enough that she'd considered marrying the guy, but they were in a committed relationship off and on for a couple of years. She'd forgiven the first transgression, but the second? That's when she'd kicked him to the curb and decided she was finally going to look for someone she could get serious with.

She laughed to herself. That person had been Zach, and now look at her. Serious didn't begin to cover it when she'd ended up with a baby.

It was Wednesday evening, and Ilsa was home alone with Mia while Holly and Rex were out having a date night. They went out a couple of nights a week, just the two of them, and while Holly had told her that was normal for them, Ilsa suspected her friend had told her a little white lie. They were used to their privacy, and no matter what Holly said, Ilsa knew it was an adjustment for them to have her and Mia living with them.

Ilsa busied herself with dishes and laundry and then took Mia to the bathroom where she gave her a bath in a baby tub. Mia loved baths and spent her entire time wiggling around in excitement and staring at the water animals that Ilsa conjured to entertain her. When the dolphins started jumping, Mia squealed and reached for them. Ilsa laughed and conjured a few orcas and sea otters to join in the fun.

After the bath was done, Ilsa swaddled her child in a baby blanket and brought her back into the living room, where Ilsa watched the latest Christmas movie on Netflix while Mia snoozed.

Just before eight, she heard the roar of an engine in the driveway and frowned. Holly and Rex were planning on dinner and a movie. She wasn't expecting them back until after ten. She rose from the couch and went to look out the front window.

A black BMW was parked next to her car, and the man walking up the steps had a very familiar gate.

Ilsa jerked the door open and stepped out onto the porch. The man climbing the steps was just as handsome as ever with his slightly wavy dark blond locks that were perfectly styled and his strong jawline that made him look like a cover model. "Kevin? What the hell are you doing here?"

He paused on the top step and blinked at her. "That's not a very welcoming greeting. Hello to you, too, Ilsa."

She tugged her sweater around her to stave off the cold and glared at him. "How did you know I was here?"

"Your cousin told me." He moved closer, reaching as if he was going to pull her into a hug.

Ilsa stepped back, putting space between them. "So you ran into Jenny, huh? Where was that? The same bar where she spotted you with that blond woman?" She hated that she could hear the bitterness in her tone. It would be much better if he thought she just didn't care at all. Not that she wanted him back. She most certainly didn't. Ilsa was one hundred percent done with Kevin Loman.

"No." He pressed his lips together in irritation. "And I already told you, nothing happened with the blonde."

"Right. Just like nothing happened with the redhead or the tennis player or the wife of your coworker's client."

"Ilsa," he said, taking a step back and bowing his head. "That's not fair. We weren't even together during most of those incidents."

She scoffed. "*Most.*" He was right, though. They weren't together when he had the affairs with the coworker's client or the tennis player. But both had happened within days of them deciding to take a step back from their relationship to see what they both wanted. Ilsa had already forgiven him once for the transgression with the redhead. There'd been no ambiguity there. He'd cheated on her and blamed it on the long-distance nature of their relationship since he lived in Marin county and she lived in Christmas Grove. She'd been furious, but he'd apologized and spent weeks trying to get back into her good graces. Once she'd relented, things went downhill fast. Then her cousin had found him in a bar trying to get the blonde's number. He'd maintained his innocence, but she knew when she was being gaslighted and had ended things between them for good that night.

"None of this matters. We're not together anymore, so there's nothing to discuss," she said.

"Oh, I think there is." His eyes flashed with a challenge that made her nervous enough that she wished someone else was home.

"What are you talking about? I haven't seen or heard from you in over a year."

"The phone works both ways, Ilsa. When exactly were you going to tell me?"

"I don't know what you're talking about. You should go." She was angry now and just about ready to call the Christmas Grove police station to have him removed from the property if he didn't leave on his own.

"My daughter? You didn't think you should tell me that we have a kid?" His eyes were narrowed, and he was staring at her incredulously.

"*Your* daughter?" she stressed, her heart suddenly racing with the idea that he thought he had any claim on Mia. "Have you lost your mind? Mia isn't yours, Kevin." Thank the gods for that.

It was his turn to scoff. "Really? You expect me to believe that? You were the most loyal girlfriend I ever had. I don't believe for a second that you cheated on me. I want to see my daughter. *Now.*" He started to push past her, but Ilsa put her arms out, blocking the doorway.

"She's not yours," Ilsa said again, this time with steel in her voice. "You have no business here and if you don't leave, I will call the cops. Understand?"

They stared each other down, and the fact that he didn't speak right away told Ilsa that he knew he didn't have any legal standing to demand to see Mia. And if she called the cops on him, it would look very bad if the partners at his law firm found out about it.

"I'll get a court order," he finally said.

"You can try." Ilsa raised one defiant eyebrow. "You're not on the birth certificate. We're not, nor were we ever, married. Nor do you share DNA, so I highly doubt you'll get very far." Even though everything she'd said was the absolute truth, he was a lawyer and that meant he had connections. If he wanted to, he could make her life hell for a while until the courts determined that he had zero parental claim on Mia.

"I will be getting a court order for a DNA test," he spat out.

She shrank back into the house, needing her space from him. "You do whatever it is you think you need to do. But answer me this, Kevin. Why do you want to see her so badly? You don't even want kids. I don't get it."

His gray eyes bored into her for what seemed like minutes but was likely only a few seconds. When he finally spoke, he said, "Because she's mine."

Kevin spun on his heel and stalked off the porch toward the car he'd bought only because he knew it would impress his father.

"She isn't yours," Ilsa called to him.

He paused at the driver's door and looked up at her. "I think she is. And when those results come in, pack your bags, because you're both moving in with me." He slipped into the car and peeled out of the driveway, leaving her with her mouth hanging open in utter shock.

Then it dawned on her why he'd come to find her. Ilsa was the one thing he wanted that he couldn't have. Mia was just a way to get to her.

A shudder ran through her. Had Kevin always been that controlling? That manipulative? That cruel?

Probably, but he'd been careful to hide it from her. He'd only shown that side of himself when he didn't get what he wanted, which had been rare in their relationship. Since they dated long distance, they'd both had a lot of freedom. They'd met when he was working for a client that lived in the next town over. It had been an intense case that required him to be in the foothills for three months. But after the case was finished and he'd moved back home, Ilsa had spent a lot of time doing whatever he'd wanted when they were together. And since he knew how to be charming and attentive, she hadn't seen him for what he was: a narcissist who would do anything to get what he wanted.

All she could do was thank the gods that she'd never agreed to marry him. She could only imagine what a nightmare that would've been.

With her pulse racing from the confrontation, Ilsa shut the door and locked it and then picked up her sleeping child. Mia's sweet face fortified her determination to make sure that Kevin never came near her daughter. Because he was a lawyer, she knew there was no time to waste.

After bundling Mia up, Ilsa grabbed her own jacket and the pair took off for Zach's house.

CHAPTER TWELVE

Zach placed the heavy box of books down in Mia's room and turned to smile at Lily. "Thanks. I'm sure when she's old enough, Mia will love these."

Lily leaned against the doorjamb with her arms crossed over her chest. "No, thank you. I know it's premature, but Evan has outgrown them, and it was either bring them here or try to find a place to donate them, which, believe it or not, was turning into a major hassle. The library didn't need them, and the nearest used bookstore is over fifty miles away."

"Hey, I'm thrilled to have them. I can't wait to start reading to Mia. Even if she's not ready, I am." He grinned at her. "Is Evan with your dad again tonight?"

She shook her head. "No, he's at a friend's house working on a Christmas art project for school. They are having an art show and Brent's mom is helping them set up in the morning, so it just made more sense for him to sleep over."

"A rare night off then?" Zach asked.

"Yes. And what did I do? I decided to use it to organize my

walk-in closet. That's where I found these books." She let out a tinkling laugh. "I'm pathetic, aren't I?"

He chuckled. "Not at all. Just a busy mom. Come on, let's get you a drink. I think you're long overdue."

Zach led the way to his kitchen where he offered up a bottle of red wine.

"Perfect," she said.

"You're showing me up, Paddington." Zach poured two generous glasses of the wine and handed one to her.

"How's that?" She put the glass to her lips, closed her eyes, and took a sip. A moment later, she let out a very contented sigh. "I think I might have just fallen in love."

Zach laughed. "I'll send a bottle home with you as a thank you."

"I knew there was a reason I liked you."

They stood in the kitchen for a few moments, sipping their wine, until Zach said, "Let's go into the living room. I'll start a fire and we can relax."

"Sounds perfect."

Spruce bounced up out of his dog bed and followed them into the next room. It was chilly since Zach had just gotten home when Lily arrived with the books she wanted to pass on to Mia. "Are you hungry? Did you get dinner?" he asked her as he worked to get a fire started in his fireplace.

Lily let out an embarrassed laugh. "I had cereal."

He glanced back at her. "Really?"

She nodded. "When I decided to take the night off, I went for it. Cooking was the last thing I wanted to do."

Zach pulled out his phone and said, "What do you like on your pizza?"

"You don't have to do that."

"Yes, I do. I'm hungry, and since you're here, we might as

well get something you like, too."

"Chicken and sun-dried tomatoes?" she asked hopefully.

He laughed and shook his head. "It's my fault for asking, isn't it?"

"Yep." She leaned back into the couch, smiling into her wine. "But if you're not into it, I can just eat whatever you get."

"Nope, chicken and sun-dried tomatoes it is." He placed the order and then sat next to her, putting his feet up on the coffee table. "This is good. It's been a long day."

Lily glanced over at the corner and said, "It's funny that Mr. Christmas hasn't even decorated his tree yet."

Zach followed her gaze to the large Douglas Fir standing in front of his window. "I haven't really had time."

"We have time now," she said, her eyes flashing with excitement. "I'm happy to help."

He waved a hand. "You're taking a break. Drinking wine. Waiting for pizza. You shouldn't have to do anything but relax. It's your night off, remember?"

She got to her feet, still holding her wine. "But I like decorating." She nudged his leg with her knee and added, "Come on. Let's do this before someone else sees this tragedy."

They spent the next hour decorating his tree, only stopping briefly to have a couple slices of pizza before they got back to it.

"I think this topper is the last thing," Lily said, holding a glass angel.

"Looks like it." He gestured to the stepladder he'd retrieved so that they could decorate the top half of the tree. "Will you do the honors?"

"I'd love to." Lily climbed onto the ladder and secured the angel on top and then twisted to look at him. "How does it look?"

"Twist it a little to the left."

She did as he asked.

He clapped his hands together and said, "Perfect."

Lily smiled at him and moved to step down, but her foot slipped, and she let out a cry as she started to fall.

"Whoa, there," he said, grabbing her waist and pulling her to him to keep her from crashing to the ground.

Lily managed to get her feet under her and turned to look up at him. "That was a close one."

"Yeah," he answered. "Are you okay?" He stared down at her in concern, wanting to make sure she hadn't twisted anything.

"I'm just about perfect, Zach," she said. And then before his brain could catch up with what she was doing, she bounced up onto her tiptoes and pressed her lips to his.

Zach froze, taken completely off guard, and then quickly stepped back. "I'm sorry, Lily. That's not—I'm not—"

The door slammed open, revealing Ilsa, who was clutching Mia's baby carrier. "Not dating, huh? What do you call this?" Her gaze scanned the room, lingering briefly on the wine bottle that was sitting in the middle of the coffee table next to the pizza box. "You know, Zach, you could've just been honest with me." Her eyes closed for just a moment before she let out a frustrated growl that sounded a lot like *asshole,* and then she turned and rushed off his porch.

"Oh, hell," Lily whispered. "I just completely messed up. I'm so sorry, Zach. I'll just go." She rushed over to the coatrack and grabbed her jacket. "Tell Ilsa I'm sorry. I didn't know you two had something going on." She grimaced. "That was not why I came over here. It just… happened."

Zach nodded at her. "It's all right." It wasn't all right at all, but what else was he supposed to say?

"I should go." Lily hurried out the door, and Zach didn't

stop her. He had to find Ilsa and clear up the massive misunderstanding.

"Lily?" he called from the front porch.

"Yeah?" she said as she was opening her car door.

"I'm sorry. We can still be friends, right?"

"Um, sure."

Zach didn't miss the grimace on her face as she hurried into her car. He watched as her taillights disappeared down his driveway, and then he grabbed his jacket and cut through the trees to the rear of Holly's Victorian.

As usual, the kitchen light was on, illuminating the space. And from his spot on the porch, he could see Ilsa pacing back and forth, her hands fisted as she muttered to herself. Mia was in her carrier on the kitchen table, eyes wide as she watched her mother, but the baby remained silent.

Zach took a deep breath and knocked on the door.

Ilsa froze.

"It's just me. Can we talk?" Zach called through the door.

"Just go away. I'm fresh out of patience for liars this evening." She grabbed the baby carrier and stalked out of the room.

"Dammit," Zach said and knocked again. "Ilsa, I'm not leaving until we talk. There's been a misunderstanding."

The mother of his child stormed back into the kitchen and flung the door open. "You expect me to believe that I didn't see you kissing Lily? That you didn't tell me that you weren't dating anyone? That I'm not the biggest fool who ever lived? Come on, Zach. You've already lied to me once. Isn't that enough?"

Her face was blotchy, and her entire body was shaking. Zach wanted to take her in his arms and soothe her, but he wasn't stupid enough to believe that she'd permit him to touch her. Not considering how angry she was. "I'm *not* dating Lily," he said firmly. "That is not a lie. I've never dated her. I'm not dating her now. And I don't intend to date her."

"So she's just a friends-with-benefits type thing then? Is that the technicality?" she spat out.

The desire to laugh was right there beneath the surface, but Zach held it back. If he did that, he thought she might lose control and deck him. But she was so far off base it was almost humorous. "Not at all. Listen, Lily came by to drop off some books for Mia. They're hand-me-downs that Evan has outgrown. From there we had pizza, and she insisted on helping me decorate my tree. It was innocent."

Ilsa narrowed her eyes and placed her hands on her hips. "Until you fell on her lips."

"Until *she* kissed me," he said quietly. "I wasn't expecting it. And I certainly wasn't looking for it." He reached out and gently brushed a lock of her dark hair out of her eyes. "I think it's pretty obvious that the only person I want to be kissing is you."

She let out a humorless laugh. "Yeah, I've heard that one before."

An alarm went off in his head. Someone had betrayed her trust in the past, and that meant he had an uphill battle to convince her that he was all in with her... not Lily. "Listen, I honestly thought that Lily and I were just friends. That we both felt the same way. I probably should've realized that the books were mostly an excuse to come see me, but I didn't until it was too late. I'm sorry you thought I lied to you. I wouldn't do that."

Ilsa stood there staring at him, a pained expression on her face. Then she blew out a breath and dropped into one of the kitchen chairs. "I hate this feeling."

He sat in the chair next to her. "What feeling?"

"The one that makes me second guess my instincts. The one that says you're telling the truth but then is overtaken by the one that's stolen my ability to trust." The pain in her voice nearly broke him.

"Ilsa..." he started, but then he didn't know what to say. How could he convince her that he was telling the truth? "I have never lied to you. That is one thing I can say with total conviction. I may have been an idiot when I stepped back from our relationship last year, and I was likely naïve about why Lily wanted to spend time with me, but I don't lie. I've been on the other end of that, and know what it feels like to be betrayed. I just want you to know that you can trust me."

There was silence between them. Zach ached to say more, to tell her how he really felt about her, but he knew she needed time and space. Instead, he pushed his chair back and stood. "I'm going to head home. Call or stop by if you want to talk. Otherwise, I'll be here in the morning to get Mia."

Zach had just reached the back door when Ilsa said, "Wait."

He turned to look at her. "Yeah?"

"There's something I need to tell you. It's the reason I came by your house tonight."

"Okay." Zach returned to the kitchen table and took his seat. "I'm listening."

She bit her bottom lip and started shaking again.

"Ilsa, what happened?" This time he couldn't stop himself from reaching out and taking her hand. "It's okay, you can tell me."

She sucked in a deep breath. "I had a visit from my ex tonight."

"That Kevin guy?" Zach asked.

Her eyes widened in surprise. "Yeah. How'd you know about him?"

He gave her a soft smile. "Your mom might have mentioned the lawyer she hoped you'd marry before you hooked up with the loser Christmas tree guy."

"She called you a loser?" Ilsa gasped out.

"Not in so many words, but it was implied." He shrugged. "Whatever. I bet the lawyer was really boring in bed." He winked, making her laugh.

"I'm not going to comment on that. Kevin was... let's just say he's a selfish man."

"I see. And he came to see you, why?"

Ilsa stared at the table and in a low voice said, "He ran into my cousin, who mentioned I have a daughter now. He came all the way up here from the Bay Area demanding to see her. And when I refused, he said he'd get a court order."

Zach's blood started to boil at the idea that some other man thought he had a right to see his daughter. "Why, Ilsa? Does he think he's her dad?"

"He's not!" she insisted. "I swear to you, he isn't. Of that I'm sure."

Zach thought about the letter he had folded up in his wallet and nodded. "I believe you."

"But yes, *he* seems to think he's her father." Ilsa slumped, hanging her head over her hands. "He won't stop until he gets what he wants."

The anger was turning into something darker, more primal. Zach forced himself to keep his voice as neutral as possible when he asked, "What does he want?"

"Ultimately?" she asked, raising her head and staring him in the eye. "I think he wants me back and will try to use Mia to make it happen. He has connections, Zach. And he won't be afraid to use them. He's talking about demanding a paternity test."

"Okay. Let him ask for one. It won't help."

She eyed him suspiciously. "You're that sure that there's no chance he's the father? Do you really trust me that much?" Her question was more astonished than curious.

"Yes and no." He reached into his back pocket, retrieved his wallet, and then pulled out the sheet of paper he'd been carrying around for over a week. After unfolding it, he placed it in front of her and gave her a self-satisfied smile. "There's no chance he's the father. I've already got the proof right here. So don't worry about whatever Kevin tries to do. He's not going to get anywhere."

Ilsa studied the paternity results for a long moment. When she finally met his gaze, there was relief shining in her eyes. But then, just as quickly, it vanished and was replaced by disappointment.

"What is it, Ilsa. This is good news, right?" She couldn't possibly want that jackass to be the father, could she? That just didn't add up, but he couldn't understand what he'd said that would cause her to be disappointed.

"Yeah. It's good news, Zach. Except for the fact that you said you'd never lied to me." Her tone was stronger now, full of fire.

"I didn't lie about anything," he said, bewildered.

She tapped the piece of paper. "You went and got a paternity test and didn't even tell me about it. That meant you needed Mia's DNA. Did you take her with you? Because I was never aware of such an outing. You didn't ask me if I thought it was okay or tell me anything about it, did you?"

Oh hell, he thought. There were a lot of reasons why he hadn't told her, but now definitely wasn't the time to get into his past and all of his traumas. "You offered a paternity test the first day I met her," he hedged.

"You're right. I did. And you know what? If you'd told me you wanted one done, I would've agreed. I would've even gone with you. But you didn't." Her emotionless gaze bored into him as she added, "And now you've lied to me by omission. I think it's best if you go now. I need time to think."

Zach didn't move from his spot at the table. There were so many things he wanted to say. To blame it on his past. On her mother for sowing the seeds of doubt. Or on her for not telling him for months. But the truth was he should've told her. She was Mia's mother, and she should've been made aware that he was taking her to the clinic for a DNA sample. The swab had been harmless, but that wasn't the point. Ilsa had deserved to know. Finally, he sighed and got to his feet. After grabbing the paternity results, he moved to the back door and paused. "We should contact a lawyer about this, get them to preemptively cut Kevin off before he starts dealing with the courts."

"Yeah, probably," she said.

"I have someone I can call. Do you want me to do that in the morning?"

She ran a hand through her long dark hair and nodded. "Yes. I think that's best. Goodnight, Zach."

"Goodnight, Ilsa." Zach closed the door gently behind him, and with his hands shoved in his pockets and his head hunched over, he made his way back to his house where he sat on his couch and stared at the twinkling tree. It wasn't long before he was on his feet, removing all of the decorations, the lights, and finally the angel.

Once the tree was bare, he shoved the bins of ornaments behind the tree and then went to bed where he lay awake all night, staring at nothing.

CHAPTER THIRTEEN

*Z*ach woke early with Spruce snuggling beside him in the bed. It was just after six when he first peeked at the clock. A smile curved his lips as he got up and started preparing to pick up Mia. The last couple of days had been brutal with Ilsa giving him the cold shoulder, but his little girl never failed to lift his mood. It wasn't until he was slipping his phone into his pocket that he saw the text from Whitney and realized it was Saturday and Ilsa didn't need him to pick up Mia.

Disappointment washed over him, followed quickly by irritation as he read Whitney's text.

Be here at nine. We need to talk.

He texted back. *Can't. There's nothing to talk about. Besides, I'm working. Busy season.*

Zach had been at her beck and call for nearly six years. It wasn't until March of this year that he'd finally started to put some much-needed personal barriers in place. He'd stopped going over to her place every Saturday. That had pissed her off, but not as much as when he'd stopped responding to every text and request for help around her house. The house he'd helped her buy and maintain.

A pipe is leaking under the sink. I need you to look at it.

He cursed under his breath and typed back, *Call a plumber.*

Guilt tried to force its way into his consciousness, but Zach shoved it back down where it belonged. For too long, Whitney had taken advantage of him. And he'd let her do it. He'd had his reasons, so he'd overlooked the demanding texts, far too few thank-yous and too little appreciation, and done what he'd needed to do. But he was over that now. She wasn't helpless, and he was done being taken advantage of.

There's no money for that.

He gritted his teeth. It would probably take him less than ten minutes to fix a leaky pipe if he had the materials he needed. Likely, it was just a seal. But it would take half his day, and he'd probably end up in another fight with his ex, and he was tired of fighting.

He wanted to just ignore her altogether, but he knew he wouldn't. That wasn't his nature. The only person he'd ever managed to ignore was Ilsa, and look where that had gotten him. *Is there water gushing all over your floor?*

No.

Put a bucket under it and then call the plumber on payday.

What if it gets worse?

Zach drummed his fingers on his counter for a few moments before typing back, *Text whoever you're dating these days if that happens.*

You're a jerk.

Zach supposed he was, but he felt that in this situation, he was entitled. After silencing texts from Whitney, Zach made a pot of coffee, filled his thermos, and then called Spruce to his side before heading out to his office. The chilly air stung his exposed skin, and he could see his breath in the air. The morning was perfect with the light dusting of snow on the ground along with the peaceful silence. It was the type of morning that filled his mind with hope and possibilities. It was the type of morning when he used to find his mother out on the front porch, wrapped in one of her crocheted scarves and fingerless gloves, watching the sunrise with a contented smile.

He wondered if he'd ever have a wife who felt as happy and content as his mother had at their farm.

Ilsa's pretty face swam in his mind. Was there a chance she'd forgive him for not telling her about the test? He hoped so. Despite the way she was currently freezing him out, he still wanted her. He'd admitted that to himself about five minutes after leaving Holly's the other night. But there was nothing to do but wait her out until she was ready to let him back in.

He'd always thought of her as more city than country, despite the fact that she'd grown up in Christmas Grove. It hadn't surprised him when she moved to Sacramento in January. There were more opportunities for managers to grow their careers. So when she moved back, that had shocked him. Or at least it had for all of two seconds before he'd gotten the biggest shock of his life in the form of Mia.

He felt a smile tug at his lips as he thought of his daughter. It was strange how she'd taken hold of his heart almost instantly. It hadn't taken long for him to get accustomed to his new reality and absolutely relish the time spent with her. While it wasn't actually all that convenient to have a baby to care for while running the tree farm, he just liked having her around. She'd become a really cool office companion. His only complaint was that he had to give her up every day. He'd like to be able to tuck her in at night, watch her sleeping face, and be there when she woke up.

Spruce followed Zach into his office and immediately found his bed in the corner while Zach sat down at his desk and turned on the computer monitor. The screen flashed with a sweet picture of Ilsa and Mia. Ilsa was staring down at her with such a look of devotion, while Mia's eyes were bright and engaged as she watched her mother. His heart squeezed almost painfully, and instead of getting to work on the previous day's deposit, he grabbed his coffee, called to Spruce, and took off through the trees straight to Holly's house.

The scent of bacon and maple syrup acted as a homing beacon as Zach and Spruce neared Holly's back porch. Spruce ran ahead of him, barking excitedly and wagging his long yellow tail. The dog knew exactly what that smell meant. He'd be glued to Rex's side all morning until the man fed him what remained of his breakfast. Zach had tried to talk his friend out of feeding his dog scraps from the table, but Rex had insisted that uncles get to do whatever they want, and Zach had conceded the argument. If Rex wanted to put up with a begging dog for the rest of his days, that was his business. Spruce knew better than to beg from Zach at home.

"Spruce, you crazy dog. What's got you up so early?" Rex called from the back porch as Spruce nearly jumped into his arms.

"He knows a mark when he sees one," Zach called back. "He sniffed out the bacon all the way at our house."

Rex chuckled. "Sure he did." When Zach reached him, Rex clapped him on the back. "It's about time you got here. Breakfast is just about ready."

"Were you expecting me?" Zach asked, tugging his coat off and hanging it on one of the pegs near the back door.

"No," Ilsa said at the exact same time Holly and Rex said, "Yes."

Zach laughed, refusing to let Ilsa's surly mood affect him. He moved into the kitchen to give Holly a kiss on the cheek. "How's my favorite neighbor this morning?"

"Good now that everyone's here." She winked at him and then shooed him over to the table. "Go sit with Mia. I think she missed you this morning."

Zach made a beeline for his daughter, who was whimpering in her baby carrier that was sitting on the table. Her face was blotchy, and her eyes were wet. "Hey, sweetheart," he said as he picked her up and pressed her to his chest. "What's got my girl so upset this morning?"

She snuggled against him and let out a sigh.

"You've got to be kidding me," Ilsa muttered, shaking her head.

He glanced over at her and raised one eyebrow. "What?"

"All morning, every time I picked her up, she just cried. The only time she settled was when I was feeding her or when she was in that carrier." Ilsa slumped back into her chair and picked up a mug that looked like hot cocoa. "Has she been this grumpy in the mornings all week?"

"Nope," Holly and Zach said at the same time. Then they both laughed.

"I think she missed her routine," Holly said. "This little one is usually on the go by now."

Zach patted Mia's back. "Yeah. We have busy mornings with our walk, then our car ride into town to see mommy." He winked at Ilsa. "She's like her daddy. Early riser with places to go and people to see."

"I guess so." Ilsa eyed them for a moment before rolling her shoulders and relaxing. "Or maybe she just missed your voice."

Ilsa's statement hung in the air, making Zach close his eyes and savor it. Had Mia missed him? He wanted that to be true more than he'd ever wanted anything. At the same time, he didn't want his daughter to be upset every morning he wasn't around. If only he'd been able to talk Ilsa into staying with him. At least Ilsa seemed to be talking to him again. It was progress.

"Don't worry, sweetie. Daddy is always just a short walk away," Zach whispered to her.

"Is this a regular occurrence? You coming over for breakfast on the weekend mornings?" Ilsa asked him.

"Huh?" He glanced up to see her staring at them. "Um, no. Sometimes. I was working last weekend."

"Most times. The only reason he hasn't been here more is because it's busy season at the farm," Rex said, rolling his eyes. "Otherwise our bacon bill would be through the roof."

"That's because you feed most of it to Spruce." The dog was pressed against Rex's leg and licking his chops as if Rex had already fed him a bite or two.

"Hey, a dog deserves his share," Rex insisted.

The morning was full of banter and plenty of laughter as the four of them gorged themselves on Holly's waffles and bacon. Zach ate one-handed, holding Mia the whole time as she dozed in his arms. By the time breakfast was finished, Zach was reluctant to hand Mia over. Hell, he was reluctant to do anything other than just hang out with a more agreeable Ilsa and his two friends. He was more relaxed than he'd been in ages. Life just felt... right for once.

"Want to go for a walk?" Ilsa asked him. "We can take Mia and let her get a little bit of her routine."

Completely taken aback by her olive branch, he grinned at her and said, "Sure." After tucking Mia into her carrier, the two of them took off with the stroller out into the clear crisp day.

Neither of them spoke for a while as they made their way

down Holly's long driveway. There was a lot he wanted to say. That he was sorry. That she wasn't the only one with a past that made her distrustful. Then there were the things like he wanted to kiss her but knew it wasn't a good idea. That he wanted her and Mia to move in with him but that would be crazy to voice right after reaching a tentative peace. That since she'd brought Mia into his life, he'd been happier than he'd ever been. But it wasn't the right time for any of that. It was too soon. So he settled for, "How's work?"

She smiled at him. "Better than I ever imagined." Ilsa spent the next half hour raving about how much she liked making potions and animated treats for Mrs. Pottson's gingerbread houses. "The magic centers me. It makes me feel like this gift has a purpose or something. I don't know. That probably sounds dumb since all I'm doing is making potions, but if one of them helps someone fall in love or have a good day, then that's bringing joy into their life, right?"

"Ilsa?" he asked.

"Yeah?"

He turned to her, feeling as if he was handing her his entire heart. "Are we okay?"

She bit her bottom lip and nodded. "I'm sorry. I overreacted the other night. I know you had every right to get that paternity test, I was just... freaked out by Kevin and not in a good place. Do you forgive me for being so cold? Especially after you took care of the lawyer. I heard from her yesterday. She said there's nothing more to worry about with Kevin. It's clear Kevin has zero claim on Mia."

"She called me, too. That's a weight off the shoulders," Zach said.

She nodded.

"Ilsa, there's nothing to forgive. You did nothing wrong. It was a stressful night. Emotions were high. I get it. And if you say we're good, then we're good."

"We're good." Ilsa gave him a shy smile.

Zach reached out and slipped his hand over hers, holding gently enough that she could pull away if she wanted to. He was gratified when she squeezed, holding on tighter. "As for what you said about your work, it's not dumb at all. It's using your gift to help someone else. We'd all be better off if all witches thought that way."

Ilsa gazed up at him. "We'd all be better off if all witches were more like you. How many 'raffles' do people win at the tree farm every week?"

He shrugged and then flushed, letting her praise curl through him like a warm hug. "However many are needed," he said.

Ilsa leaned in close and brushed her lips over his cheek. "You're a good man, Zach."

He'd heard people say that to him before, but he'd never really thought much about it. He was just doing what he'd been raised to do. "Dad always said we were lucky in life and it was our job to pay it forward. So that's what I do. It's not that big a deal."

Ilsa stopped underneath a large pine tree, forcing him to stop, too. She turned into him, pressed her palms to his cheeks, and said, "It *is* a big deal. It's a *huge* deal, Zach Frost." And then she kissed him.

CHAPTER FOURTEEN

*I*lsa didn't know what had come over her. One minute she was out walking with Zach, deciding she was over her snit, and the next she had her arms around him, her body pressed against his, and was kissing him like she'd die if she had to hold off for one more second.

His arms went around her, and she reveled in the way that he pulled her close, deepening the kiss that she'd started. It felt as if a year of pent-up passion was being poured into the kiss, and Ilsa wanted to stay right there forever.

But reality soon butted in when Mia let out a small cry, making it clear she missed being the center of attention.

Ilsa and Zach pulled apart, both of them slightly breathless. They both reached for Mia at the same time, but Zach got to her first, swiftly cradling her into his embrace. She settled instantly.

"What are you? The baby whisperer?" Ilsa asked, feeling both slightly annoyed and amazed at his effect on the child. "She only settles down like that once I'm feeding her."

He chuckled. "Well, I can see why she'd be impatient."

Ilsa rolled her eyes. "Whatever." But then she watched them together and felt her lips curl into a contented smile. When she let her guard down, their little unit just felt right. "Looks like you're carrying her for part of this walk."

"Not a problem." He hoisted her so that she was resting against his shoulder and then nodded to the stroller. "If you can handle that, I've got the precious cargo under control."

"You got it." They walked along the tree-lined road, talking about everything and nothing. Neither of them mentioned the kiss, and to her surprise, instead of feeling awkward about it, she just felt content. The sun was out. Her daughter was happy. And the man she'd been half in love with for years was by her side, laughing and chatting and making plans for the upcoming week. It all felt so... normal and perfect. Much better than the last few days when she'd been wallowing in self-pity.

It was well past time she started working on her trust issues. And after Lily had apologized to her, affirming that she was the one who'd kissed Zach, Ilsa had decided she couldn't hold anyone, not even Zach, to a perfect standard. She didn't even want to. What she wanted was a partner, someone to lean on, someone to love. And in her heart, she knew that person was Zach. He was nothing like Kevin, and she just needed to learn to trust her instincts.

By the time they made it back to Holly's house, Ilsa felt better than she had in weeks. The walk had energized her, but her time with Zach had lifted her mood, and she knew she'd tuck the memory of the day in her mind as one of those perfect Christmas season moments with her new family. Because no matter what happened between her and Zach, there was no doubt that he was family now.

"Oh, thank the gods, you're back!" Holly cried as she burst out onto the porch. "We have a situation."

Ilsa stiffened as all the joy she'd banked from the walk slipped away and was replaced by anxiety as she took in her friend's appearance. Holly's shirt was soaked and so was her hair. "What happened? Did you get into a fight with the shower or something?"

"I wish," she said with a huff of frustration. "A pipe burst, and before we realized what was happening, most of the upstairs flooded."

"What?" Ilsa ran into the house and nearly cried when she spotted the water running down the stairs. "How bad is it?" she asked Holly.

"Bad." There were tears in her eyes as she continued. "Your room and the second guest room are soaked. Ours has water, but I think we can get it back into some sort of shape fairly soon. But the ceiling caved in your room, ruining your bed and the crib."

"Oh no," Ilsa whispered, covering her mouth. "I'm so sorry, Holly. Your house… that's a lot of damage."

She nodded, squeezed her eyes shut, and then shook her head as if to shake off the dismay. "I have insurance. It will be okay. But it's going to take some time before either of the guest rooms are habitable again."

"That means Mia and I are going to have to go to my mother's," Ilsa said as she sank down onto the couch, feeling the blood drain from her face. It would be brutal having to listen to her mother try to control her life every single day. It would mean Zach would be subjected to her opinions on a daily basis when he picked up Mia. Her gut tightened as she looked up at him, an apology already forming on her lips.

"The offer to stay with me is still on the table," he said. "Mia already has a room. You can have my guest room. I'd offer you my cabin, but Maya's been renting it." Zach had a cabin on the family property. Rex had stayed in it before he moved in with Holly. It would've been the perfect solution.

"Thanks, but I don't think—" she started.

He put his finger up to her lips, stopping her. "Would you rather stay with Birdie?"

She shook her head.

"I didn't think so." He gave her a gentle smile. "Why don't we just try it. It was kind of a rough week, but we've worked past it, right? And it's not forever. I'll help Rex get this place fixed up and you can be back in your room here in no time."

Ilsa had to admit, even if it was only to herself, that staying with Zach sounded a thousand times better than relocating to her parents' house. Not only would she never hear the end of her mother's wishes that she'd marry Zach, she'd also be subject to numerous opinions about how she was caring for Mia. Her mother just couldn't help herself.

"It does sound better than being under Birdie's watchful eye," Holly said. Her face was red, and her eyes were blotchy. There was no question that she'd been crying.

Ilsa stood and wrapped her friend into a hug. "It will be all right. Sheetrock and ceilings can be fixed, right?"

Holly nodded. "I know. It's stupid of me to be upset. But I keep thinking about the wallpaper in your bedroom. Grandma and I put it up together. And those pale green walls in the office, she chose that color. I just feel like a piece of her has been damaged today. A piece I've been carrying around with me for years."

"Oh, honey. Those are your memories. Wallpaper and paint can be replaced, too. You know that."

Holly shuddered and pulled back to stare at her friend in horror. "You want me to replace the mauve-colored rose wallpaper in your room? Are you out of your mind? And what about that lima bean green? Do you really think that's what we should go with? Have you lost the ability to recognize tasteful decorating? Who *are* you?"

Ilsa couldn't help it; she laughed. "Okay, okay. You're right. Those design choices are at least twenty years out of date. I only mentioned you could replace them so that the house would stay the same. But I see now that you're not on board with that plan, which frankly, I wholeheartedly approve. Redecorate once the repair work is done, hold on to the memories, and know that the love that you hold in your heart for your grandmother is what keeps her spirit alive. Not a house. Not green paint. And definitely not that mauve wallpaper."

"That's better," Holly said, hugging her friend again. "Can you imagine purchasing that hideous pattern again? I imagine the salesclerk would slap my hand for even considering it."

The two laughed together until Rex appeared and said, "I see we've entered the hysteria phase of the ceilings caving in."

Holly just shrugged. "What else is there to do? I already cried about it. Can't do anything until the insurance people document it. The other choice is to drink heavily, but since Ilsa is teetotalling right now, that didn't seem wise."

Rex gave her a tired smile. "At least you've moved into the acceptance phase."

Zach handed Mia over to Ilsa and turned to Rex. "What happened? How did it get to the point of the ceiling caving in?"

"I'm not sure. Looks like the pipe burst sometime while we were having breakfast. Or maybe before that and the water built up in the ceiling. We went for our own walk after you and Ilsa left and returned to find water streaming down the staircase. It's a real mess up there."

Rex walked to the staircase. "Come on. I'll show you what I'm talking about."

The two men disappeared up the stairs, leaving Ilsa and Holly alone with the baby.

"How bad is it really?" Ilsa asked her. "Am I going to have to replace everything?"

Holly winced. "Probably." But then she perked up. "You do have some laundry in the laundry room, though. You won't have to go naked at Zach's. Well, unless you want to." She winked.

"Funny. I'm glad to see that the house destruction hasn't kept you down for too long," Ilsa said dryly.

"I'm just trying to distract myself from the fact that I won't have a working shower in the morning." Holly hung her head. "I'm really going to dislike having to take a sponge bath." She grimaced. "That's akin to torture."

Chuckling at her friend, Ilsa said, "Why don't you just come over to Zach's? I'm sure he won't mind if you use one of his."

"I guess I'll have to, but it's going to be a pain in the butt."

"Still better than a sponge bath." Ilsa patted her on the arm, tucked Mia into her baby carrier, and went to find whatever clothes she had in the laundry room.

CHAPTER FIFTEEN

"*H*ome sweet home," Zach said, dropping the two suitcases near the door. Ilsa moved past him into the farmhouse with Spruce on her heels. He still couldn't believe that she'd agreed to his suggestion of staying with him. Sure, he'd have preferred it if she'd decided on her own instead of being forced into the situation because of a busted pipe, but he wasn't going to look a gift horse in the mouth. He was just going to enjoy the fact that he got to tuck his daughter in every night and be there when she woke up every morning.

As for Ilsa, he held out hope that their relationship would continue to progress past friendly co-parents. If he had his way, he'd have Ilsa sleeping in his bed, but he knew that regardless of that kiss they'd shared earlier in the day, it was way too soon to be considering a physical relationship. Not after the last week they'd had.

Ilsa glanced around as if it were the first time she'd ever seen the place. "What happened to your tree?"

He grimaced. "It didn't feel right, so I took the decorations down."

Her brow furrowed. "It didn't feel right? It was pretty. Or at least what I remember of it."

"The person who helped me decorate it isn't the one I wanted to build memories with," he said, unable to hide the truth from her any longer. "She's here now, though, so if you decide we should do something about it, let me know."

Ilsa's cheeks flushed as she glanced away, unable to meet his eyes. But he didn't miss the small smile tugging at her lips. Her gaze lingered on the mantle that was full of family photos. It wasn't until Spruce jumped up to get her attention and nearly knocked her over with his excitement that she looked away and focused on him. "Hey there, Spruce. You're acting like you haven't seen me all day. What's up, boy? Do you need something?"

"He wants a treat," Zach said. "He always gets one when we come home from work. He's taken that to a whole new level and now demands one every time he steps in the house, no matter where he's been."

"Well, in that case, let's get you a treat, huh, boy?" Ilsa patted Zach's arm as she moved past him into the kitchen. It didn't take her long to find the container where he kept the dog treats, and instead of getting mauled by Spruce, who started to jump on her, she said, "Sit, Spruce."

To Zach's surprise, the dog immediately sat down on his haunches and waited patiently for her to feed him the treat.

"Good dog, Spruce. Such a good boy," she said and held out the treat to him. He took it gingerly, and once he had it in his mouth, he ran back into the living room and crawled into his bed where he happily chomped down on the Milk Bone.

"You're the dog whisperer. You know that, right?" Zach asked as he set Mia's carrier on the kitchen table. The baby was fast asleep and had been since before they'd left Holly's.

"He just needs a little discipline," she said.

Zach snorted. "Right. Because I never thought of that." He jerked his head. "Come on. Let me show you your room."

Zach picked up Mia's carrier and then placed a hand on the small of Ilsa's back and guided her down the hall to the first bedroom. It wasn't large, but it did have a queen-size bed and an armchair in the corner. The bed was made up with a solid white quilt and was accented with sunflower-print pillows.

"Zach," she said, smiling at him. "Did you do this?" Ilsa waved at the room.

"Um, you mean add the bed and the chair?" He chuckled. "Yeah. I replaced the old double bed that had been in here for over twenty years after a buddy and his girlfriend slept over and I spent all night listening to squeaky springs."

She laughed. "That did not happen."

"I assure you, it did. I barely slept at all with their mattress antics going on all night. Once they left, I burned the sheets and immediately ordered a new bed. It's fairly new and has never been slept on. Let me know what you think."

"I will." She glanced around for a moment and then said, "Show me Mia's room?"

"Right this way." Zach stepped into the hall and waved a hand at the room directly across from hers.

"I'm glad it's close," she said, pressing a hand to her heart. "This will be the first time she's had her own room."

"She's been sleeping in your room?" Zach guessed. He had already figured out that Mia and Ilsa had been using the same room at Holly's, but it somehow hadn't occurred to him that this would be the first time the baby was sleeping through the night without someone else in the room.

"Yes. I like having her close." She sat in the rocking chair next to the crib and picked up a super-soft plush dog. She caressed the dog's ears while she took in the room and bit her lower lip. "This room is incredible, Zach. I can't believe you did all this."

"I wanted her to know she belongs here," he said with a shrug, placing Mia's carrier beside the rocker. The baby was still sound asleep. "I didn't want to half-ass it. And I wanted you to know she'd have everything she needed if she was ever given the opportunity to stay over with me."

She lifted her gaze to meet his. "You wanted her to stay over?"

He nodded and then moved to crouch in front of her. "I love spending time with her. I think that's obvious. But I want more, Ilsa. I want to be there when she goes to sleep and when she wakes up. I don't just want to be a part-time dad. I want all of it. And I know that we have circumstances that make it so that might not be possible, but I want *you* to know that I'm very happy you're both here. I'm sorry for the way I brought it up before. That first day, when I just blurted out that you should live here, that was dumb. I was overwhelmed and not super rational. I get why you weren't running to move in here. But I'm glad you're here now, for however long that is."

Ilsa's eyes misted, but she didn't let any tears fall. She just gave him a wobbly smile, cupped his cheek with one hand and kissed the other one. "I don't love that most of our stuff got ruined and that's the reason we're moving in here, but I am ready to give this living arrangement a chance."

"Anything as long as you don't have to go to your mom's?" he teased, already feeling the tension drain from his body. He'd been worried that she really didn't want to be there with him. The fact that she didn't seem all that upset about it meant that maybe they could work on building something. Something real. Something that just might last.

"Well, there is that," she said with a grin. "But it does help that you're not hard on the eyes." She leaned in and gave him a soft kiss on the lips. Then she stood, collected Mia, and disappeared into her room.

Zach stared after them, his heart in his throat. He'd fallen in love with his daughter almost instantly. Now he was starting to think that he was falling for Mia's mother, too. Sure, he'd always been attracted to her. The only reason he'd put the brakes on their relationship before was because of Whitney. He'd liked Ilsa. Had fun with her. She made him laugh, and she was sexy as hell. But he'd never thought he was actually falling in love with her.

Now, though? Ilsa McKenzie had softened over the last months. Her heart was mostly on her sleeve instead of hidden behind her sassy mouth. She was kind, fiercely protective, and still as strong-willed as she'd ever been. He found himself admiring her and wanting to be around her. Only this time he wasn't thinking about getting her into bed every five minutes. Now it was more like he considered what it would be like to be with her again about once an hour.

What did that all mean? He had no idea other than he wanted both of them around. And if Ilsa did eventually end up in his bed, he vowed not to eff it up this time. Because he desperately wanted to feel her soft curves against his body again, run his hands over all of that smooth skin, and kiss her absolutely everywhere.

His entire body heated with the idea of having a naked Ilsa in his bed with him, and he couldn't help the groan of frustration that slipped between his lips. It was the first night she was under his roof, and he was already fantasizing about her in his bed. He needed to get a grip.

His instinct was to follow them into Ilsa's room. Instead, he went into his kitchen, pulled some chicken out of his freezer, and went to work.

CHAPTER SIXTEEN

*I*lsa wrapped her lips around the fork and moaned in appreciation as the savory sauce hit her tongue. She'd spent most of the afternoon in Mia's room, reading to her daughter and playing with her on the floor. It wasn't often that Ilsa was able to just devote her undivided attention to Mia without worrying about what she was supposed to do next. While living at Holly's, she done everything she could to make her friend's life easier. Since Holly wouldn't let her pay rent, Ilsa had paid her back in other ways, like doing laundry, vacuuming, and doing the dishes.

She'd have offered to cook, but unfortunately, Ilsa wasn't the best cook in the world. Holly was a thousand times better at it than Ilsa was, so by an unspoken agreement, they'd left the cooking to Holly.

That was why, when she scented the Italian spices in the air, she nearly drooled on herself. Zach had left her and Mia alone for the afternoon, and now she knew why. Was the man a saint? He seemed to have the ability to not only help those in need to have a wonderful Christmas, but to also be the perfect father and housemate, because there was no question what he was making in that kitchen of his.

After tucking her daughter into the crib, Ilsa made her way to the kitchen and stood leaning in the doorframe as she watched Zach work his magic. The man was a culinary genius. Or he was as far as she was concerned. Her idea of dealing with dinner was to order on Door Dash.

"Zach Frost," Ilsa said, standing with her arms crossed over her chest. "Who taught you to cook?"

He looked up and smiled at her. "My mom. It was one of her mandatory skills that both her kids were required to learn. She said if we could cook, we could survive anything."

Twenty minutes later, she was seated at his table with a plate of chicken marsala, steamed broccoli, and an Italian salad in front of her. "The chicken is delicious," she said after savoring a bite. Using her fork to point at the broccoli, she added, "You know, I was ready to throw you under the bus for serving me broccoli, but the chicken has more than made up for your attempt to force vegetables on me."

His eyes sparkled as he raised his glass of red wine in her direction, clearly wanting to toast to something.

"I'm not drinking remember?" she said, ignoring his toast.

"That's why I gave you sparkling water. Are you really going to leave me hanging here, McKenzie?" He had one eyebrow cocked and was still holding the wine glass up.

"Oh, I guess not." She raised her glass to his and asked, "What are we toasting to?"

"To new beginnings and to the future," he said.

"Kinda vague, don't you think?" she said and then took a sip of her sparkling water.

"Not vague at all," he challenged. "We both know what I'm

talking about, but if you want me to spell it out, I'm more than happy to do that."

She choked and shook her head, massaging her throat.

He laughed. "You're adorable, you know that?"

"Adorable?" It was her turn to cock an eyebrow. "Nobody has ever called me adorable before. I'm not exactly the cuddly type."

"That's a lie. I have reason to know otherwise," he said, digging into his chicken.

Her lips twitched with amusement. "I guess you do. But I meant figuratively. In real life, I'm pretty prickly. It doesn't take much for me to challenge someone if they've annoyed me. Or to speak up when I think someone is suffering an injustice. But give me a gorgeous man to share a comfortable bed with and yeah, I can be persuaded to cuddle. You've got me there."

He gave her a look that implied he might be interested in testing out exactly how much she enjoyed a gorgeous man in her bed, but he didn't say anything. Just nodded his agreement.

Ilsa wanted to scream, and she didn't know why. Was it because he hadn't taken the bait and insisted that she sleep in his room that evening? Or was it because she was annoyed at herself for not taking him up on his offer to live with him the first time he'd said it. It was definitely the former. Ilsa loved bantering with him.

Still, she remained animated through dinner, asking him about his childhood, his parents, his brother. He enjoyed talking about them and told some old stories about him and his brother as kids. They'd been inseparable, and Zach didn't feel like he had one significant memory that didn't include his brother Dane.

"There was this one Christmas when a couple with a little red-headed girl showed up two days before Christmas to pick out their Christmas tree. Dane and I were about fifteen and sixteen," Zach said as he started another story.

"Little red-headed girl? Seriously? What is this, the Charlie Brown Christmas?" Ilsa teased.

"Almost. They tried to pick out the smallest and cheapest tree, but my dad wasn't having any of it. He insisted on giving them the largest one that would fit on their van, and he only charged them for the small tree that would've definitely needed Linus's blanket to keep it upright."

"It's good to know the apple doesn't fall far from the tree," Ilsa said, grinning at him. "Your dad sounds like he was a wonderful guy."

"He was," Zach said softly. "But that's not the point of the story. You see when Dane and I spotted the redhead at the same time, it became an all-out war to one up each other to see who could win... hell, I don't know. Her approval? It wasn't like either of us were going to date her. They lived sixty miles away. And at that age, it's a dealbreaker. Anyway, we spent the entire time showing off, cutting each other down, and then devolved into an all-out fight over her. We were rolling around in the snow, ready to kill each other, and by the time our dad broke it up, the redhead was gone."

Ilsa threw her head back and laughed. "You two deserved nothing less."

"No doubt about that," he said, chuckling. "So imagine my surprise when she wrote a letter a few weeks later addressed to me."

"No!" Ilsa pressed a hand to her mouth. "What did it say?"

"That she was sorry she couldn't spend any time getting to know me. That she tried to wait around to give me a goodbye kiss, but after her father saw us rolling around like idiots, he hadn't wanted his daughter to be a part of any of our nonsense. Which, again, made sense."

"So you missed out on kissing the red-headed girl because of male ego?" she asked, leaning forward with her elbows on the table.

"That's right. And not only did I miss out on kissing her, I missed out on my very first kiss *ever* because of Dane. The bastard." Zach's smile grew to a grin and he shrugged again. "My brother never let me live that down. I got my revenge, though, when I told the girl he liked that he had herpes."

"You didn't!" Ilsa stared at him with her eyes wide.

"Hell yes, I did. She believed it and told a couple of her friends, which turned into an epic rumor mill. From then on out, he had the uphill battle of convincing all the girls that he didn't have the virus and he was in fact safe to date."

"Oh, Zach." She pressed her hand to her mouth and giggled. "I heard that rumor. I had no idea it was because of you. That's brutal."

"It was," he said with a nod. "But he had people convinced that I failed an IQ test, so it wasn't as if he was innocent either."

"I'm so glad I was born a girl," she said.

His gaze swept over her, and he nodded in agreement. "Me, too."

Ilsa felt herself flush. It was time to exit the conversation unless she was prepared to just jump him and get it over with. He'd made her a fabulous dinner, had been charming as hell, and now he was flirting with her.

Abort, abort, abort.

"Uh, I should get the dishes done," she said, clearing their plates and heading to the sink.

"Ilsa, no. You don't have to do that," he said, following her.

"Yes, I do." She turned around to face him. "You cooked. That means I clean. It's the only fair way."

There was such a finality in her tone that Zach just raised his hands in the air in a surrender motion and said, "All right, McKenzie. If you must do the dishes, I'll let you. But you can't stop me from clearing the table."

Gods, he was fun to be around. "I wouldn't dream of even trying."

Once the remnants of dinner had been put away and all the dishes were done, Ilsa went to check on Mia. The baby was still crashed out, appearing to not have moved a muscle while she was sleeping. Ilsa already knew it was going to be a volatile night. No way was she sleeping through it after a nap like that. At this rate, she'd probably want to feed at least twice in the middle of the night.

While Ilsa loved the way that breastfeeding had helped them to bond, it wasn't her favorite thing in the world. It would be especially brutal if she had to feed Mia while she was half asleep.

When Ilsa didn't return to the kitchen right away, Zach came looking for them.

"Mind if I join you?" he asked when he poked his head in.

"Of course not," she said, waving him over to watch Mia sleep. "Look at her. Isn't she gorgeous?"

"She looks like you," he said.

There was that flush again. How was it he had the ability to change her from wholesome mommy to the woman who couldn't wait to tear her clothes off within two seconds flat?

"There it is," he said softly. "Gorgeous." He touched her face with one hand and added, "I love when your cheeks turn pink. Just really effing gorgeous."

Things were going to get out of hand fast if Ilsa didn't take charge of the situation. The way he was looking at her and the way her body was responding was too much, too fast. She hadn't even spent one night in his house, and she was ready to jump right into the sack with him. It was time to regroup.

Ilsa cleared her throat. "I think I'm going to get Mia ready for bed and then turn in myself. Thank you again for taking us in and for the fabulous dinner. You have no idea how much I appreciate it."

"You're welcome, Ilsa," he said, holding her gaze. The mixture of seriousness and lust was quite the combination, and she felt as if she could hear his thoughts running around in his brain. He wanted her just as much as she wanted him, but neither of them was going to let it happen. He leaned in, brushed his lips over her cheek, and then retreated. "Let me know if either of you need anything. I'll be right down the hall."

Sure. Because that's a good idea. Not. Now all she was going to think about was what he was or wasn't wearing in the giant bed of his that was just a few feet away from her own room. "Yeah. Okay. Goodnight, Zach."

"Night, Ilsa."

CHAPTER SEVENTEEN

*Z*ach woke to the sound of the baby crying. He squinted at the clock beside the bed. It was just past two in the morning. Groaning, he rolled out of bed and pulled on a pair of sweatpants.

He stepped out into the hallway and followed the dim glow of light into Mia's room. Ilsa, wearing red flannel pajamas, was holding Mia, pacing as she tried to calm her. "Hey," he said softly.

She turned and said, "I'm sorry we woke you."

"Don't be sorry. This is what parents do." He gave her a tired smile and moved in to caress Mia's pink cheek. "Hey, little one. What's with all the drama?"

Mia's cries only intensified.

"Now you've done it," Ilsa said, shoving her slightly mussed hair back behind her ear. Up close, it was hard to miss the dark smudges under her eyes that indicated she wasn't getting enough sleep.

He yawned and stretched his arms out. "Want me to try for a bit?"

"Yes," she said kind of desperately. "I haven't been to sleep at all."

Frowning, he took the baby in his arms and patted her back. "She hasn't been crying all night, has she?"

She shook her head. "No. I had trouble getting to sleep, so I came in here to watch her for a while. When she woke up, I fed her right away, hoping that would satisfy her and put her back to sleep. But no such luck. She napped for about twenty minutes, got a diaper change, and is now just annoyed with the world, apparently."

"I can see that." Zach kissed the top of Mia's head, but her cries just kept coming. He took a seat in the rocker, and as soon as he started to move, her cries turned to whimpers.

"Oh, thank the gods," Ilsa said, sighing in relief. "I tried that, but..." She shrugged. "I guess you have the magic touch."

"This time," he said with a small smile. "The other day she serenaded me for an hour before we finally came to an agreement."

"Yeah? What was the agreement?"

"She wanted to lay on my chest as she napped." Zach rubbed Mia's back. "But not here. On the couch." Mia squirmed and let out a short wail. "Shh, love. It's okay."

The baby's lungs opened up and the crying filled the room.

"Oh goodness, Mia," Ilsa said with a grimace. "Glad to know your lungs work."

The crying was so loud, Zach's ears were starting to hurt. He got to his feet, still holding Mia to his chest, and said, "Time to try the couch."

He grabbed one of the baby blankets out of the crib and made his way into the chilly living room. Because of the glass sunroom on the far end of the house, the main living room was always cooler than the bedrooms at night. He draped the baby blanket over Mia, laid down on the couch, and then pulled the extra blanket off the back to cover his lower half.

Ilsa curled into the adjacent chair, watching them.

Mia calmed down almost instantly, and Zach let out a sigh of relief. There was nothing more frustrating than not being able to soothe a crying baby.

"Looks like you've figured out the secret." Ilsa covered her mouth as she yawned so hard that her eyes started to water.

"You should go back to bed and get some sleep," he said.

"Not just yet." Her gaze swept over him and Mia. "I want to just take this in for a minute."

Warmth spread in his chest as his heart beat just a tick faster. The tenderness in her gaze did things to him. It made him feel things he'd never felt before.

"Why are you looking at me like that?" she asked with a nervous laugh.

"Like what?" he asked.

"I don't know. Like you have a secret you're not sharing… yet." She glanced away, and even though it was dark in the room, he guessed she was blushing.

"Ilsa?"

"Yeah?"

"I do have some secrets. And at some point, I definitely want to share them with you. But right now, I'd rather lie here and just enjoy this moment with my family." *My family.* The words had come out of his mouth without any input from him. His first instinct was to retract them, but he couldn't. They were the truth. Mia was his daughter, and no matter where his relationship stood with Ilsa, she was the one he wanted by his side for however long she'd let him into her life.

"Your family, huh?" The lightness in her tone told him that

she didn't mind that he'd claimed them. In fact, she seemed happy as she smiled at him.

"Yeah." His voice was hoarse with emotion, and he cleared his throat. "You know what would make this moment better?"

"What's that? Some heat?" She curled into herself and rubbed her arms to warm up.

"I was going to say Christmas lights on the tree, but a fire in the fireplace would do it." He started to swing his legs over the edge of the couch and sit up.

Mia instantly started to cry.

"Whoa there, you two. Lay back down," Ilsa said. "I'll handle the fire and turn on the tree lights."

"That would be great, except there aren't any lights on the tree," Zach said with a yawn.

"What?" She glanced over at the tree. "You took those off, too?"

He shrugged one shoulder. "Lily insisted on white lights. I like the flashing colored ones. They remind me of my mom. You know the saying, 'less is more'?"

"I might have heard of it," she said with a slight laugh.

"My mom hated that saying. She always changed it to more is more. More color. More lights. More pizzaz. That was just her nature." He stared at the undecorated tree. "It just didn't feel right without them."

"I get it," Ilsa said softly as she placed a Firestarter log in the fireplace and lit it. The fire came to life without any more effort from her. After a moment, she added a few more logs and then closed the glass door. She stood there watching the fire flicker for a few moments and then walked over to the bare tree. The bins of decorations were stacked up in the corner behind it. "Are your colored lights in there?"

He nodded. "Yes. Maybe tomorrow I'll get the lights on it."

"Why not right now?" She smiled at him and then dug into the boxes.

"Ilsa, it's late. Don't you want to get some sleep?"

"I will... eventually." She pulled out a couple of boxes of colored lights and quickly got to work stringing them on the tree.

"I hate that I'm not helping you with that," Zach said, his fingers itching to get to work. He wasn't one to watch while someone else did his work for him.

"Zach, you're doing exactly what I need you to do right now. If Mia's happy, I'm happy." She quickly finished with the lights, adding them as high as she could reach, and when she sat in her chair again, the they were flashing happily on the tall tree.

"It's perfect, Ilsa," he said softly.

"It's easy to be comfortable in your house," she said, tucking her feet underneath her.

"It's your home, too. For now at least."

She stared at him, her blue eyes sparkling in the firelight. "You're a good guy, Zach Frost. Thank you."

"I'm just a guy who wants to spend time with Mia and her mother," he said. Ilsa was so lovely in the dim light that Zach was dying to reach out and touch her. But she was too far away and moving wasn't an option. Mia had finally passed out, and he wasn't going to do anything to risk waking her.

"It's more than that," Ilsa said. "We both know that."

He gave her a short nod. Of course she was right. He wanted to do a lot more than just spend time with Ilsa, but in that moment, he was perfectly content just bonding with his daughter. "Tell me what I missed."

She frowned. "What do you mean? Tonight, while I was trying to get her to sleep?"

"No. What it was like when you were pregnant, Mia's birth, and the two months of her life that I missed. I want to hear about it." It was something he'd been thinking a lot about. Was her pregnancy easy? Had she been excited? Nervous? Terrified? Was it an easy birth, or did she spend three days in labor? And how did she survive on her own for two months with a newborn?

"Oh." Her voice was soft. "You really want to hear about all that?"

"I really do. I hope you know by now that I'd have been there for you every step of the way if I'd known what was happening."

"I see that now. At the time..." She let out a sigh. "When I first found out and you didn't call me back, I was a mess. I was angry, a little bit terrified, and also really happy."

Hearing her talk about how he'd ignored her made a lump form in Zach's throat. If he could go back and change his actions, he would in a heartbeat. The choice he'd made was one he'd regret for the rest of his life. "I'm so sorry, Ilsa. You have no idea how sorry I am."

She gave him a sympathetic look. "Actually, I kind of think I *do* know how sorry you are. And just so you know, I wouldn't have brought it up except that you wanted to know about that time. It's just my truth. But I don't want to keep throwing it in your face. Mistakes were made. I'm to blame, too. I could've driven up here and knocked on your front door. It's not like I didn't know where you were."

"Thank you for saying that, but you aren't to blame here. I am," he said, knowing how much he'd hurt her. He was unwilling to do it again.

"Let's just not do the blame game anymore, okay?" she

asked. "It's our history, but we don't need to carry it around with us every day. We can leave it in the past. Deal?"

"Deal." He watched her, letting it sink in just how amazing she was. Just how different she was from Whitney. His ex's face flashed in his mind, and he quickly pushed the thought of her aside. There was no room for her when he was with Ilsa.

"After I got over my initial shock and anger"—she gave him an apologetic smile—"I got really excited. And I loved being pregnant. I just felt... I don't know, like I could do anything?" She laughed a little. "And once I could feel Mia moving, I lived for those moments. It was just a really special time. Or it was, until my back started to ache all the time and I had to pee every five minutes."

Zach grinned at her. It was obvious she was reveling in those memories, but hearing about it felt like a gut punch. He wished he could've rubbed her back for her and talked to his daughter while she was still in the womb. "Would you do it again?"

Surprise flashed through those pretty blue eyes of hers. "Um... maybe?" Her expression turned to one of mirth. "Why? Are you offering?"

He laughed. "I'm up for trying if you are."

"I bet." Shaking her head, she rolled her eyes.

"Seriously though. If you were in the right circumstances, would you want another one?" Zach didn't know why he was asking. Or rather he did know, he just wasn't willing to admit it, even to himself.

"That's a deep question for the middle of the night, Zach." She snuggled into the chair, closing her eyes. After a few moments, she whispered, "Yeah. I think I would."

"Me, too," he whispered back. He stared at the dwindling fire, imagining a life with her and a couple more kids. The idea sparked joy that tingled over his skin. He imagined them all running around the Christmas tree farm and sitting around the dining room table as they celebrated. His mind wandered to what it would be like to fill the house with kids, and he mentally started thinking about extra bedrooms. It was a wild fantasy, and not one he'd had before. Sure, he'd wanted a family, but his thoughts hadn't ever moved past a wife and one kid. Now he could see an entire future with the woman sitting across from him, but he was certain he couldn't tell her what he wanted. Not yet. It was too soon.

"Zach?" she asked sleepily.

"Yeah?"

"I'm a little cold. Is there another blanket?"

"In my room. Top shelf of the closet," he said, moving to get up again.

"No. Stay there," she said, blinking her sleepy eyes at him. "Don't wake Mia. I'll get it." She pushed herself out of the chair, wobbled a little bit, and then slowly made her way down the hall.

Zach waited for her to come back, but when minutes ticked by and he couldn't hear her moving around, he decided he had no choice but to check on her. He sat up slowly, careful not to wake the baby. Though there likely wasn't much chance of that. He'd spent enough time with her to know when she was completely conked out. Nothing was going to wake her up at that point.

After stopping in the nursery to put Mia back to bed, he grabbed the baby monitor and went in search of Ilsa. Her room was empty. So was the bathroom. He continued on to his room and stopped in the threshold and smiled when he spotted her on his bed wrapped up in a fleece blanket. Her mouth was slightly open, and she was breathing heavily.

Zach sat down on the edge of the bed and brushed her hair back. "You and Mia look a lot alike when you sleep," he whispered.

Ilsa stirred slightly, opened her eyes once, closed them, and reached out one hand to grab his wrist. "Time to sleep, Zach," she muttered.

"Yes, it is." He leaned down and pressed a kiss to the top of her head.

Her eyes fluttered open and she gave him a soft smile. "Sorry, I didn't mean to fall asleep here. Just so tired."

"I know. It's fine. Go back to sleep." He started to move away again, but she pulled him back.

"Stay," she muttered as her eyes closed again. "Please."

He glanced at her wrapped up in his blanket and chuckled softly. Sleeping next to her while she was in her cocoon wouldn't hurt anything, right? He quickly grabbed another blanket from his closet and climbed onto the bed on the other side. After spreading the blanket over himself, he curled up next to her back and said, "Good night, gorgeous."

She reached back, grabbed his hand, and tugged it over her waist so that he had no choice but to spoon her.

He didn't resist. Instead, he tugged her closer, pressed a kiss to her neck, and promptly went to sleep with her cocooned body pressed up against his.

CHAPTER EIGHTEEN

*I*lsa woke suddenly, her eyes flying open and making her squint in the morning light. She rolled over and nearly rolled right into the man sleeping soundly next to her. She froze and then glanced around the room.

Zach's room.

Oh, no. What had she done?

She vaguely remembered wandering into his room the night before to get a blanket. Then she'd decided she was too tired to do anything else and crawled into bed. But she wasn't entirely sure she realized she'd crawled into Zach's bed. She'd been exhausted after being up half the night with Mia.

Mia.

Ilsa tried to swing her legs over the side of the bed but was stymied by the blanket that was wrapped around her. She looked down at herself and almost laughed. Whatever she'd been worried about happening the night before, it was clear she didn't have anything to be concerned about. A chastity belt couldn't have worked better.

It took her a moment to untangle herself, and she was just

getting up when Zach reached out and lightly grabbed her wrist. "Where are you going?"

She glanced back at his sleepy eyes, mussed hair, and bare chest. Goodness, he was sexy. "To check on Mia."

"I did that about an hour ago. She's sleeping." His husky morning voice sent a tingle up her spine. "Come here," he said as he tugged her back down and wrapped an arm around her, pulling her close.

"You checked on her an hour ago? And I didn't hear you?" she asked, shocked she hadn't woken up.

"You were sleeping pretty hard." His eyes had cleared, and he was staring into hers with intensity. "I didn't want to wake you."

Ilsa's insides turned to mush. "You know what, Frost?"

"What's that?"

"If you keep taking care of Mia during the night, I'm never going to want to leave."

His lips curved into a self-satisfied smile. "Good. And it only took me one night."

She chuckled, but then her breath caught as his gaze dropped to her lips. Her entire body flushed with heat as the tension between them went from zero to sixty in an instant.

"I'm going to kiss you now," he said.

"Okay," she breathed.

Zach's hand tightened on her waist as he tugged her closer, and his warm lips brushed lightly over hers. Her eyes fluttered closed, and she was ready to sink into him when a squawk came from the baby monitor.

Ilsa let out a tiny groan as she pulled away. "Someone's awake and ready for breakfast."

"Not just yet," Zach said. Then he pulled her back to him, and this time when his lips met hers, he kissed her thoroughly, leaving her slightly breathless when he finally pulled away. "Now that's a good morning kiss."

Ilsa pressed her fingertips to her lips and grinned. "I'd say so."

Mia let out another squawk, followed by a demanding cry.

"Time's up," Ilsa said. "The little one calls." She kissed Zach on the cheek and rolled off the bed. "Thanks for letting me sleep. I needed it."

"You're welcome." He stretched out on the bed, his arms over his head, exposing his muscled bare chest. The view was almost enough to get her back over to the bed, but when Mia's cries turned to something slightly above bloody murder, Ilsa abandoned her fantasies and hurried down the hall into the nursery.

After Mia was fed, changed, and back in Zach's care, Ilsa retreated to shower and dress for the day. When she finally emerged, she found Zach holding Mia against his chest while he hung a variety of hand-painted ornaments on the Christmas tree.

"Those are pretty," she said, peeking into the box.

He smiled at her. "My mom painted them."

"They're gorgeous." She picked one up that had a horse and carriage parked by the Christmas Grove river. "You didn't put these up when Lily was here." It wasn't a question, but a statement.

Zach shrugged. "Doing the tree was her idea. I hadn't even gotten these out of storage yet. I suppose that is part of the reason it didn't feel right."

"I can see that." She took Mia from him and cuddled her.

"It's not the only reason, though." Zach put the box of ornaments down and moved to stand in front of her. "Decorating the tree was always a family thing around here. It was often chaotic, and no one agreed on anything, but it was always the four of us. I haven't decorated my tree with family around for a few years now, and I wanted this year to be different."

Ilsa understood exactly what he was saying. "You wanted Mia to be a part of it."

He nodded. "And you."

Her heart fluttered. He was going to kill her. She just knew it. Ilsa stepped into him, pressed her palm against his cheek, and kissed him softly. "Thank you, Zach. I can't think of a better gift."

"I can," he said, letting his gaze roam over her before he laughed and then winked at her.

"Stop." She rolled her eyes. "Your daughter is right here."

"So you're saying there's a chance then." He nodded. "Got it."

Shaking her head, she stepped away from him and started moving toward the kitchen. "I'm making breakfast. What are the chances you have any eggs?"

"Great. I have farm fresh eggs. But I don't think you're going to need them."

"Why's that?"

"You'll see." He led the way into the kitchen and retrieved a tray of food from the oven.

"Waffles?" Ilsa cried. "You made waffles!"

"You don't need to sound so surprised. This isn't the first time I've cooked for you," he said good naturedly. "You were busy getting all prettied up after taking care of Mia. I figured it was the least I could do."

"That was really sweet of you. Thanks."

"Just you wait until I collect payment." He winked at her.

"Payment, huh?" She eyed him suspiciously. "What did you have in mind?"

He pulled a couple of plates out of the cabinet. "Oh, I don't know. How about I get control of the remote and no complaining when I want to watch Die Hard for the hundredth time, because it's the only acceptable Christmas movie out there?"

She threw her head back and laughed. "You're a piece of work."

"I'm the piece of work who made you waffles and bacon." He pulled a second tray out of the oven that was full of bacon. After plating their breakfasts, he carried them to the table where butter and syrup had already been placed.

"You're something else," she said, taking her seat and chewing on a piece of bacon. "Thank you."

"You're welcome. We make a good team, wouldn't you say?"

"Yes." It was amazing to her that she'd been in his house for less than twenty-four hours, but they were already in sync. How was that possible?

They bantered back and forth about meal planning for the following week, discussed who'd do the dishes, and who was getting up in the middle of the night when Mia cried. Zach had agreed to a fifty-fifty split of household duties, but when she went to do the dishes and he shooed her away, she knew their lives would never be fifty-fifty.

Zach Frost was a nurturer, and it was clear to Ilsa that he quite enjoyed being needed. If they stayed together in the same house, she was willing to bet that Zach would be taking over all the meals and plenty of the diaper changing. The only thing he wouldn't be taking off her plate was breastfeeding Mia. Although, Ilsa thought if Zach could do that, he'd do it for sure.

"You're going to spoil me," Ilsa said, staring at him as he loaded the dishwasher.

"Is that a bad thing?"

"No." *Yes.* If she ever planned to live on her own again, now she'd know what she was missing.

"That's what I thought. Now, go bundle Mia and get your jacket on. It's time for a walk."

She raised an eyebrow. "Are you ordering me on a walk?"

He laughed. "Me, order you to do anything? No. But take a look outside. I don't think you're going to want to miss this."

Ilsa turned and stared out the windows of the sunroom and then let out a gasp of surprise. "Snow!"

It wasn't the first snow of the season, but it was the first one that had actually dropped more than just a dusting. If they went out, they'd probably need snowshoes.

"You told me once that you and your dad always used to take walks together after the first snow. I figured you'd want to keep the same tradition with Mia."

Oh, hell. Her stupid heart was going to beat right out of her chest. Was it possible this man, the one who'd dumped her so abruptly last January, really was as sweet as he appeared to be? She knew he was a good man. That was never a question. But his ability to know what she needed at all times was the thing that could break her if whatever they were doing didn't work out.

"Go on," he said gently. "Get ready and bundle up Mia. We have a walk to take."

CHAPTER NINETEEN

The air was clear and crisp as Ilsa, Zach, and Spruce walked among the Christmas trees on the Frost farm. Zach had surprised Ilsa when he produced a wrap-around baby carrier. After he tucked Mia against his chest, they'd walked outside, strapped on their snowshoes and headed into the trees. Spruce ran ahead of them, his feet barely touching the snow in his excitement.

It was Sunday morning, usually a busy time for the farm, but with the fresh snow, the plows hadn't been out yet and the morning was still filled with silence.

"I can't believe you had that carrier." Ilsa glanced over at him and shook her head. "You're full of surprises."

"I'm a busy man during the day, Ilsa. And this little one goes with me everywhere while you're at work." He smiled at her, enjoying her reaction. "It took a bit of research to find the right one, but she seems to like it."

"I can see that."

The fresh snow made for an easy walk with the snowshoes, and they took their time walking the perimeter of the farm and then found themselves in the clearing behind Holly and Rex's place. Spruce ran up onto the back porch and jumped up on the door, desperate to see his aunt and uncle. Or more likely to see Rex, his bacon dealer.

"Hey, bud," Rex said, opening the door to the yellow beast. "Did you miss me?" The dog jumped up on him and licked his face. "Ew. Okay, I guess that's a yes," he said with a laugh.

"Good morning," Zach called.

"Morning, neighbor." Rex waved, and Holly appeared, joining him on the back porch.

Zach and Ilsa made their way to the back porch and ditched their snowshoes.

Holly held her arms out and made a grabby motion with her hands. "Give me that baby. It's been too long since I've had my Mia time."

"We haven't even been gone twenty-four hours," Ilsa said.

"Shush, you. Mia and I have some catching up to do," Holly said as Zach handed her the baby. She cradled the child against her chest and whispered something before pressing a kiss to the top of her head.

"Holly's missed her morning ritual with Mia," Rex said, opening the door and waving them in. "I think she might need a puppy if you end up staying at Zach's." He chuckled, but no one else did. "What?"

Holly rolled her eyes. "A puppy? Really?"

"What's wrong with puppies?" he asked, looking bewildered.

Rolling her eyes, Holly took Mia and disappeared into the other room. Ilsa hurried after them, leaving the men alone with Spruce.

Rex glanced at Zach. "What did I do?"

"Dude," Zach said, shaking his head. "Get a clue."

Rex stared at the doorway with his brow furrowed. It wasn't long before he turned back to Zach and said, "I totally just stuck my foot in it, didn't I?"

"Yep. It's no secret to anyone that Holly desperately wants babies," Zach said with an air of sympathy. "I don't think she appreciated the puppy crack."

Rex sat at the table and ran a hand through his light brown hair. "Damn. I'm an idiot."

Zach briefly clasped a hand on his shoulder. "Sorry, man. But I'm sure you can smooth this over."

"Yeah, sure."

Zach left him in the kitchen with Spruce and went into the living room. Ilsa and Holly were sitting on the couch, Mia in Holly's lap.

"He wants to wait until after we're married, but we haven't even set a date yet," Holly said. "Which means I have no idea when any of this is going to happen. It's driving me insane."

"Waiting until you get married isn't unreasonable," Ilsa said, meeting Zach's eyes and giving him a sheepish smile.

He returned it and moved to stand at the end of the couch where he could be closer to her.

"Your friend is an idiot," Holly said to him.

Zach laughed. "At least you're both on the same page."

"What's that supposed to mean?" Holly asked, obviously way too upset to parse his joke.

"He just acknowledged that fact right before I came in here. He may be slow sometimes, but he still manages to catch on." Zach glanced behind him to see Rex was standing in the doorway. "Sorry," he said to Rex.

"Don't worry about it. You're right." Rex turned his attention to Holly. "Do you think we could talk for a second?"

"I'm visiting with Mia," Holly said, her tone cold.

"Come on, Hols," Rex said, giving her a tiny smile. "You don't want to miss my groveling, do you?"

Holly met his gaze, and immediately her chilly exterior started to thaw as her lips twitched.

Yeah, that tiff wasn't going to last long. Zach had never met two people who cared about each other as much as Holly and Rex. When they'd finally come together, they'd been all in, one hundred percent committed to each other. In fact, Zach was surprised the wedding date hadn't been set. He wasn't sure what his buddy was waiting for. Holly was his perfect match.

"Here. I'll be right back," Holly said, handing Mia off to Ilsa.

"Take your time," Ilsa said. "I think Zach and I are going to take Mia to go check out your holiday display."

That was news to Zach, but he assumed Ilsa wanted to give the couple some privacy so they could talk without their friends listening in.

"Just don't leave without letting me say goodbye, okay?" Holly leaned over and kissed Mia's head.

"Of course not. Besides, Spruce is still in the kitchen," Ilsa said.

"Probably eating half the contents of the refrigerator," Zach muttered.

"I'll send you the bill," Rex called as he followed Holly into the other room.

"I bet he does, too. That dog has probably eaten his weight in bacon," Zach said.

Ilsa chuckled as she stood and started moving toward the front door. "Let's go."

Zach was skeptical they could get to the holiday display, which was quite a way down Holly's driveway, but he was proven wrong when they stepped out onto the porch. It looked like Rex had already cleared their driveway. He briefly wondered if his buddy had taken care of his private drive and the one at the tree farm, too.

"Come on," Ilsa said, her eyes sparkling with mischief as she handed him Mia and then took off down the driveway.

Zach tucked his daughter into her carrier and smiled as he watched Ilsa. There was a lightness in her step and a general ease about her that hadn't been there before. She looked... content, happy, relaxed. His chest expanded with warmth and happiness. If he could capture that moment in a painting, he would. But it had been years since he'd tried his hand at painting, and he'd never been as good as his mother. Instead, he took out his phone, quickly snapped a photo, and slipped it back into his pocket.

"Hurry up. You're lagging behind," Ilsa called just as she rounded the bend in the driveway.

He chuckled to himself and hurried to catch up with the woman who was responsible for bringing joy into his life in the most unexpected way. After rounding the bend in the driveway, he saw her standing in front of the large magic-filled tent.

The year before, Holly and Rex had erected a Christmas hall with long tables, multiple Christmas trees, floating candles, and an area where kids could be sorted into houses. It was also a designated place to drop off toy donations for underprivileged kids for the holiday season.

"Can you believe they put in all of this work?" Ilsa asked with awe in her tone. "Those two have so much going on already, and yet, here they are giving back to the community like it's just no big deal."

Zach knew exactly how much work it was to put up the large tent and get other people to help them with the magic. He also knew that Holly loved it and Rex lived to make Holly happy. "It was such a success last year. I imagine the town would be pretty sad if they didn't do it again this year."

"Yeah. I guess." Ilsa moved into the tent and let out a gasp. "Look! That's new." She pointed at portraits on the wall, all of them of various people in town: Mrs. Pottson, Lemon Pepperson, and Lily Paddington. Ilsa recognized each one as someone who had helped putting the display together. The portraits themselves were striking, but what made her gasp in delight was that they were moving in the frames. "Who do you think made that happen?"

"I have no idea," Zach said. He moved in behind her and placed one hand on her waist while he pointed to the adjacent wall with the other. "Look."

Ilsa let out a gasp. "Holly painted all of us."

The wall was lined with portraits of Ilsa, Zach, Mia, Rex, and Holly herself. There was also one of Amelia, Rex's sister. None of them were moving, though. Instead, they had perpetual snow falling in the background.

"Holly outdid herself," Ilsa said, and Zach thought he heard a catch in her voice.

"Mia is lovely," Zach whispered in her ear.

"She is." Ilsa wiped at her eyes and then turned to face him. "She painted her family."

"I know." Holly's parents passed away when she was still a child, and she'd lost her grandmother when she was a young woman. That left Ilsa, Rex, and now Zach, Mia, and Amelia as her chosen family. Zach was just as touched as Ilsa.

"Holly's amazing. I hope Rex gives her a child soon," Ilsa said, still dabbing at her tears.

Zach chuckled. "I doubt that's going to be an issue. You know how he is. It just takes him a little time to come around to things."

Ilsa nodded. "I know. I just hope it's sooner rather than later."

"You just want a playmate for Mia," Zach teased.

Her smile told him that he wasn't that far off.

"I'm having a really good day, Ilsa," he said.

"Me too." She pressed up on her tiptoes and brushed her soft lips over his.

He would've loved to lean in and deepen the kiss, but with Mia between them, a make-out session wasn't really in the cards. When they pulled apart, he asked, "If you aren't busy tonight, what do you say to a date? Dinner? Maybe some mini golf?"

"Mini golf? Have you lost your mind?" she said with a laugh. Their first date had been a double date with Holly and Rex at the arcade where they played mini golf, and Ilsa hadn't exactly proven to be a golf pro.

"Nope. I just want an excuse to put my hands on you," he said. "That swing of yours could use some work."

"I was just nervous," she insisted.

"I know." He cupped her cheek with his palm and caressed her cheekbone with his thumb. "What do you say?"

"I'll need to ask Holly if she can watch Mia," Ilsa said and then bit her bottom lip.

"Considering the way she practically snatched her out of my hands earlier, I'd say the chances are good." He nodded toward the house. "Let's go find out if they've made up."

It didn't take long to return to the house, and when they got there, Holly and Rex were sitting on the porch swing with Spruce at their feet. They had a blanket over their laps, and both had mugs of hot chocolate.

"Holly," Ilsa gushed. "Those portraits. They are fabulous."

Holly flushed and leaned into Rex. He put his arm around her, confirming that they'd made up. "You like them?"

Ilsa rolled her eyes. "Like them? I love them. You outdid yourself."

Holly beamed. "Thanks."

Zach cleared his throat. "Holly, I was hoping you could do me a favor tonight."

She raised one eyebrow. "Tonight?"

He nodded. "If you're not already busy, I was hoping you could watch Mia for a while. I'd like to take Ilsa out on a real date."

Holly glanced between Zach and Ilsa, and then a huge smile broke over her face. "You two are sleeping together again, aren't you?"

"Holly!" Rex said with a laugh. "Subtle."

She shrugged. "Just look at them. They are both way too relaxed."

Zach met Ilsa's gaze and smiled at her when her lips twitched. She put her arm around his waist and leaned into him with a familiarity that made his heart soar as he said, "We're not sleeping together. Not that it's any of your business."

"Actually, we slept together last night," Ilsa said in a matter-of-fact tone.

"I knew it!" Holly pumped her fist.

"I mean, we actually slept," Ilsa said, batting her eyelashes. "Sleep is sacred when you have a baby around. So when I crawled into his bed in a sleep-deprived delirium and he found me there asleep, he let me be. And for that I am ever grateful." She slipped her arm around him and tugged him closer to her. "So I figure he deserves a date. But only if we can find a sitter for Mia."

"I'm in. I'll watch her," Holly said excitedly. But then she frowned as she glanced back at the house. "Except all of her stuff that's here is ruined."

"I'll bring what she needs," Ilsa said, both nervous and excited. She wasn't nervous about leaving Mia with Holly. Far from it. She was nervous because Zach had asked her out, and the last time he'd done that, she'd been a complete fool. Surely she was used to him by now, right?

Ilsa twisted into him at the same time he turned into her, and just like she'd done a year ago on their first date, her hand got in the way and she accidentally grabbed his crotch. "Oh, no." Her hand flew to her face, covering the mortification she knew had to be etched over her features. "I'm sorry. I did not intend to do that."

Laughter spilled from her porch mates, and when she finally got the courage to look at Zach again, his eyes were full of amusement. "Looks like nervous Ilsa is back. I can't wait to find out what else you grab tonight."

She couldn't help it. She threw her head back and laughed.

CHAPTER TWENTY

"Can you believe that Holly went out and bought a new crib today?" Ilsa asked Zach as he led her into Pine Needles. The place had the best pasta in town and a mean tiramisu that Ilsa had been craving for weeks.

Zach laughed. "Yeah. I guess I can. Though, if they really are going to try to start a family, I guess it's not a completely crazy purchase. It means she can keep Mia overnight and when or if you move back, you won't need to buy another one for a while."

Ilsa's throat went dry. His casual talk of Mia staying overnight with Holly made her second guess her decision when Holly had offered to take her for the evening so that she and Zach could "get some sleep." She'd used air quotes and everything. Ilsa had reluctantly agreed, but she made Holly promise to call her if Mia was fussy or if there was any sign of anything that wasn't quite right. It wasn't a trust issue. It was a new mom worrying too much issue.

She was also unsure about moving back to Holly's house. Ilsa had only spent one night in Zach's home, and she was already convinced that she should stay. Zach wanted her to. She wanted to. And there was no doubt that Mia loved having her daddy around as much as possible.

"Hey. What's wrong?" he asked.

"Oh, nothing. Just thinking about Mia staying with Holly tonight." She gave him what she imagined was a wobbly smile. "It's hard to be away from her."

"We can always pick her up on the way home. Holly will understand." He wrapped an arm around her shoulder, tugging her close.

Ilsa leaned into him, sinking into the comfort. "I know. She's just so little. Last night was the first time we ever even slept in different rooms."

"I know, love," he said.

Love? Had he just called her love? She turned to stare at him, wide-eyed, but the hostess arrived just then to take them to their table.

Once they were seated, a waitress arrived and asked, "Can I get you some wine or a cocktail tonight?"

"Just water for me," Ilsa said automatically.

"Are you sure you don't want a glass of wine?" Zach asked her. "One glass isn't going to hurt."

He was right of course. Not to mention that she'd already pumped an extra supply of milk. Holly had enough to get Mia through until morning. "Yeah, okay. One glass. Something red."

Zach picked a cabernet that she'd never heard of, and then the waitress wandered off to put in their drink order.

Ilsa stared at the menu for a minute, and then she started to laugh.

"What's so funny?" Zach asked, placing his menu down on the table.

"This." Ilsa waved a hand around the dining room. "The

wine. Being out on a date. It's all just so foreign to me now. The last time I did this was… well, with you."

He reached across the table and covered her hand with his. "Do you miss it?"

She frowned. "Miss what? Restaurants and wine?"

"Not just restaurants and wine. I mean your life before Mia. You were single, free to do what you wanted. You were on a different career path. I just wondered how you feel about the life you have now versus the one you had then."

"What kind of question is that?" She pulled her hand away. "Are you trying to ask if I regret Mia? Because—"

"No. Not at all." He sucked in a breath and let it out slowly, trying to find a way to ask her what he wanted to ask without offending her. There was no way around it. He needed to go with the truth. "I've known people who, after they had their first kid, started to hate their life. It was really hard to watch. I guess they thought nothing would change and then regretted their choices."

"I don't regret anything, Zach," she said, leaning back in her chair. "How could I regret that sweet baby?"

"That's not…" He shook his head. "I know you don't regret her. You adore her. I can see that. I just want to make sure the life you lead now is one you want. If it's not, I'd like to do whatever I can to help you achieve your goals." He knew he sounded like an idiot. Despite his earlier thought that he just needed to be honest with her, there were things he hadn't yet told her. Painful things from his past that he didn't like to talk about.

"Like what kind of goals?" Ilsa asked, tilting her head to the side to study him. "My job? My living arrangements? The time I spend with my daughter?"

"I guess I mean your job, and yeah, where you live. Or if it came down to it, a nanny so you had some time to recharge." The word *nanny* left a bad taste in his mouth. He wanted the two of them to raise Mia as much as possible.

"Something's wrong," Ilsa said, studying him. "This conversation isn't about me. It's about you."

He let out a soft chuckle. She wasn't wrong. "I guess that's true. But it still doesn't change the fact that I want to make sure you have the opportunity to live the life you want. If I can help, I will."

The waitress arrived and took their orders, but Ilsa kept her gaze on him the entire time. Once they were alone again, she said, "I love my life just the way it is. It's not what I planned, no. But I love my time with Mia. I really like my job despite the fact that I'm not running the show." It was her turn to chuckle. "Though, I pretty much do my own thing every day. It's kind of nice not having to boss everyone else around."

"That's good," Zach said, noticing she hadn't said anything about her living arrangements. But what did he expect her to say? Her room at Holly's had been trashed by a busted pipe, and she'd only spent one night with him so far.

"I like where I'm living now, Zach," she said softly. "I love Holly and Rex, but it's different at your place. It's more like we're a team, you know? Holly has obviously been a huge help and loves Mia with everything she has, but there, I did all the feeding and changing and soothing when she wouldn't sleep. With you, I actually got some sleep for once." She grinned at him. "And I'm comfortable there."

Zach let out a sigh of relief, not realizing just how much he'd needed to hear those words.

"Now, what about you? As far as I can tell, you're completely content with taking care of Mia in the mornings and having her keep you up half the night."

"That's true." He nodded. "I adore her. She actually fun to have around at work, and as far as you two living with me, it's perfect. I wouldn't change a thing." It was easy for him to tell her how he felt. But talking about his past? That was something entirely different.

She nodded. "Do you want to tell me what happened in your past to prompt this conversation?"

He paused for a moment before answering. "I will, eventually, but not tonight. I want this evening to be fun. I want it to be about you, not my baggage. Is that okay?"

"Of course." To his surprise, Ilsa reached across the table and covered his hand and squeezed it. "I won't hurt you, Zach. Not like she did. I promise."

His heart nearly beat right out of his chest. Because that was the crux of it, wasn't it? He'd embraced her and Mia wholeheartedly, just like he'd done in the past when another woman he'd thought he loved needed him. And she'd hurt him. But he already knew that what he'd gone through with Whitney would pale by comparison if Ilsa ever walked away from him. Zach was falling fast and hard, and there was no way to stop it even if he wanted to.

After the wine came, Zach made a point of avoiding heavy conversations. Instead, he spent the evening flirting and throwing out innuendos. Ilsa matched him toe-to-toe, and by the time they were done eating dinner, they were both a little handsy.

"Are you still up for mini golf?" Zach asked, running a hand down her side and grasping her hip as they made their way out to his Chevy Tahoe.

Ilsa answered his touch by sliding her hand down and brushing her fingers over his perfect butt.

He pressed her against the passenger-side door, leaning in

and whispering, "If you keep doing that, we're never going to make it to Karma Arcade."

She was staring at his lips when she said in a husky voice, "That's fine by me."

Zach wanted to growl, to cover her mouth with his own, and claim her right there on Main Street. Instead, he leaned in, his lips an inch from hers, and said, "You're playing with fire. You know that, right?"

"Are you saying I'm going to get burned?" she asked, her fist curling in his sweater as she tried to pull him even closer.

Holy hell, she was going to be the death of him. "Not burned, but if we do this, I think we're both going to go up in flames. Are you ready for that?"

"Yes," she said and then pushed him away as she added, "Take me home, Zach. I've been waiting for this for almost an entire year."

That was all he needed. He quickly opened the door for her, and once she was in, he ran around to his side and jumped in. But before he started the engine, he leaned over, took her mouth, and kissed her with all the pent-up passion of a man who'd been starving for her ever since he'd recklessly walked away from her.

CHAPTER TWENTY-ONE

*I*lsa was lost in Zach. His lips were locked over hers, and she'd let go of all of her fears and inhibitions. She wanted him. Wanted him more than she'd ever wanted anyone. Her heart was hammering in her chest, and her skin tingled from his touch.

She reached out and buried her hands in his thick dark hair, and when he pulled away slightly, she let out a contented sigh.

Zach smiled tenderly at her.

"That was… intense," she said, caressing his cheek.

"We're just getting started, Ilsa." He kissed her again, but before she could sink back into him, he pulled away and fumbled for his keys. As he was putting the key in the ignition, his phone buzzed. He glanced at it, frowned, and then ignored it.

"Problem?" Ilsa asked.

"Nope. It's nothing to worry about." He put the SUV in gear and backed out of the space.

Ilsa's own phone buzzed. She opened the text from Holly to

find a picture of Mia sleeping soundly in the new crib. Her heart swelled as she looked at her peaceful little girl. "Mia is fast asleep."

Zach glanced at her. "Did you want to pick her up and take her home or let her stay at Holly's?"

She pursed her lips as she studied him. "What do you want to do?"

He let out a low chuckle. "Remember those kisses?"

How could she not? Her lips were still tingling. "Of course."

"I'd like to finish what we started, and worrying about Mia waking up would seriously interfere with those plans. But if you need to stop and pick her up—"

"No," Ilsa said breathlessly. "Just take me home."

Zach gave her a sexy half smile, took her hand in his, and kept his focus on the road all the way back to his farmhouse.

By the time he opened her door for her, the butterflies in her stomach had taken over, and her entire body was slightly jittery with anticipation. He didn't make her wait. He grabbed her by the hand, led her into the house, and tugged her straight to his bedroom.

They stopped next to his bed, and he immediately took her face in his hands and kissed her. He tasted sweet with a hint of coffee, and the rest of the evening faded away as she let herself get lost in him.

"I've wanted you since the moment you returned to Christmas Grove," Zach said as he pushed her coat off her shoulders.

She chuckled. "That's what you were thinking when you saw a baby in my backseat?"

"No, it's what I was thinking the moment I saw you standing in front of Holly's house. When I saw Mia, I was gutted, thinking you'd moved on. But then you said she was mine, and all I could think about was that both of you were my family and I needed to figure out how to earn your trust again." He tucked a lock of her hair behind her ear. "Did I finally manage to do that?"

"Yes." Ilsa took a step closer, ran her hand through his hair, and then divested him of his jacket. She placed her hands under his sweater, plastering her fingers on his well-defined abs.

He sucked in a sharp breath, and his stomach quivered under her touch.

She smiled up at him. "I think you like that."

"I like you touching me anywhere." He tugged his sweater off, revealing a gorgeous chest, and then went to work on stripping her out of her dress.

His hands were everywhere, and despite the cold night, her skin was on fire from his touch. This was what she'd been missing.

And when he pulled his covers back and led her into his bed, she knew everything between them was about to change, and she wouldn't have it any other way.

Just before dawn, Ilsa woke to soft caresses along her spine and let out a small moan of approval. "That's lovely."

"You're lovely," Zach said, pressing a soft kiss on her shoulder. "How did you sleep?"

She rolled over to stare up at him. "Better than I have in months."

"I guess I wore you out." He winked and gave her a cocky grin.

"You could say that. I was also more relaxed than I've been in months."

He chuckled and wrapped an arm around her, pulling her into him so that he was spooning her from behind. "I know you have to get up and go to work soon, but I just want to enjoy you for a few more minutes."

Zach felt so good next to her that even though she knew the clock was ticking, she closed her eyes and enjoyed the sensation of his lips moving over her neck and shoulder. It wouldn't be often that they got uninterrupted time to themselves. She didn't want to rush it.

It didn't take long before Ilsa was wrapped around Zach and completely lost in the moment. When they were both panting and satisfied, she glanced at the clock and groaned. "No. Dammit, I'm going to be late."

She rolled out of his bed and rushed into the shower. Five minutes later, she ran out in just a towel, finding the bed empty. Zach was up, but she didn't have time to find out why. She hurried into her room, threw on a pair of jeans and a sweater, and with her hair still wet, she ran into the living room. "I should have left ten minutes ago," she said, grabbing her purse and keys.

"Here, take this," Zach said, handing her an insulated to-go mug.

She took a sip and let out a groan of pleasure. "You made me a mocha?"

He grinned and opened the door for her. "I'm full of surprises. Now let's go. I'm taking you to work this morning."

Ilsa hurried out of the house after him. "You don't have to do that. I can drive."

"I know you can. I just want every minute I can get with you." He opened her door and then ran around to his.

As the Tahoe rumbled down the drive, she said, "You know this means you have to come pick me up, too, right?"

"Yep." He held her hand all the way to Love Potions. Just as she was about to get out of the SUV, he got a text.

"Is that Holly?" she asked, checking her pockets for her own phone. When she came up empty, she searched her purse until she found it. No new texts. No calls. She let out a sigh of relief as she glanced at Zach.

He was frowning at his phone again. "Not Holly."

"Okay. Then who? It's way too early for work to be texting."

He nodded. "It is, and it's not work. It's my ex."

A jolt of jealously hit Ilsa in the gut. "Your ex is texting you at five in the morning?"

He closed his eyes and leaned back in his seat. "It's complicated."

Her eyebrows shot up. "That's not reassuring, Zach. Why is she texting you?" Ilsa couldn't believe this was happening. She'd just let all her guards down when it came to Zach. She was ready to try again, to see where their relationship could go. She'd already given him her heart. And the morning after, his ex was texting him at an ungodly hour? What the hell was going on?

His eyes popped open and he met her gaze. "Like I said, it's kind of complicated. Can we talk when you get off work?"

She gritted her teeth and wanted to say no. Wanted to tell him that she needed answers sooner than that. But how crazy was that? She and Zach hadn't made any promises to each other. Not yet anyway. And in the couple of weeks she'd been home, she hadn't seen even a hint of an ex in his life. There was no doubt about it; she was overreacting. Even so, her voice sounded cold to her own ears when she said, "Yeah, I guess so."

"Ilsa," he said quietly, "I promise you, there is nothing going on with Whitney."

Whitney. The name bounced around in Ilsa's head, and a vague image of a gorgeous blonde with long legs, long hair, and a tiny waist materialized in her mind. Had Ilsa met her before? It was possible considering she and Zach had lived in the same town for most of their lives. She just couldn't remember if she'd ever seen them together. Ilsa pushed her door open. "All right. See you at noon?"

"I'll bring Mia by at nine," he said.

Her irritation vanished, and she gave him a small smile. "Thank you for that. I miss that sweet face."

"Me, too." He grabbed her hand and gave it a quick kiss. "I'll see you soon."

Ilsa nodded and took off at a run toward the shop. The bells rang, making her cringe. It meant the store was already open.

"Good morning, Ilsa," Mrs. Pottson said from behind the counter. Her dark hair was in a side braid, and a few tendrils framed her round face.

Oh, hell! Why did her boss have to pick that morning to come in early? In the two weeks that Ilsa had been working there, she hadn't seen her boss before 10:00 am. "Mrs. Pottson, I'm so sorry for being late. Something… ah, came up. I promise it won't happen again."

Her boss looked past her at the street where Zach was just pulling out of his spot. "I bet it did," she said with no small amount of innuendo. "Don't worry, dear. It just means that things are working out as they should."

Ilsa stared at her, speechless with her mouth hanging open. Mrs. Pottson was a notorious matchmaker. She didn't hesitate to slip people love potions if she sensed they needed it. But she hadn't given one to Ilsa. Had she? Ilsa was certain she'd have noticed.

"Relax," Mrs. Pottson said, her blue eyes dancing with amusement. "There was no need for me to slip you a potion." Her entire face lit up as she laughed. "You two sealed your destiny last year when you made that sweet baby. One doesn't need to specialize in love magic to see that."

Ilsa blew out a breath. "I'm glad you didn't slip me a potion, but the jury is still out on what our destiny is."

Mrs. Pottson studied Ilsa, her eyes narrowed in concentration. Then she shook her head. "Nope. It's already written. You'll see."

CHAPTER TWENTY-TWO

*a*fter forcing herself to put Zach and his ex firmly out of her mind, Ilsa's first couple of hours at Love Potions flew by. The weekend had been a busy one, and Mrs. Pottson had plenty of gingerbread houses that needed Ilsa's edible snowflakes and snowmen. She had fun animating the snowmen so that they did a silly hula hoop-type dance. Each time she cast the spell, she had to mimic the dance, which made her giggle.

"You're having way too much fun back here," Lily said from behind her.

Ilsa jumped at the sound of the other woman's voice. "Oh, Lily. I didn't even know you were here."

"I just got in." She grabbed an apron and tied it around her waist. "Listen, Ilsa..." she started.

"Yeah?" Ilsa wiped her hands on a towel and gave her coworker her attention.

"I just want to tell you again how sorry I am about the Zach thing. I should've realized you two had unfinished business. It's just that... well, he was so nice to me. And while he talked about Mia, he didn't really talk about you much, and I thought... Well, it doesn't matter what I thought. Now that I look back on everything, it was all in my head. He needed help with the nursery and then was nice enough to take me to dinner to thank me. I read something into it that clearly wasn't there. He's never looked at me the way he looks at you."

Ilsa blinked at her, surprised by the other woman's speech. They'd already talked about Zach once. It had been a short conversation, but Ilsa had already put that incident behind her. "You don't need to apologize again, Lily. I know it was a misunderstanding. Besides, Zach and I weren't really together then. Not *really*."

"There was something, though," Lily said, giving her a soft smile. "Right?"

Ilsa nodded. "Yes, there was."

Lily nodded and moved closer to squeeze Ilsa's hand. "After I realized I'd been reading into things on my end, it was pretty obvious he's into you. I just really like you and don't want there to be any weirdness between us."

"There's not," Ilsa said. "I promise." *Or at least not anymore.* Ilsa could admit to herself that she'd been uneasy around Lily ever since she'd spotted her kissing Zach, but the truth was that she really liked the other woman. She didn't want to be carrying around a silly grudge just because Lily had wanted to date Zach and had thought him single. Hell, half the single population of Christmas Grove wanted to date him. The man was a catch.

"Thank goodness." Lily blew out a breath. "The only close friend I have in this town is Holly, and I know she's your best friend. I was sort of hoping the three of us could hang out sometime. I know you're a new mom and busy and everything, but—"

"Yes. Let's have a girls' night sometime soon," Ilsa said. "We can get Zach and Rex to watch Mia and Evan sometime later this week. What do you say?"

Lily nodded and beamed at her. "Sounds perfect."

Ilsa grabbed a tray and loaded the finished gingerbread houses on it. She turned to Lily. "Can you open the door for me? I'm going to put these in the display."

"You got it."

Ilsa carefully carted the houses out into the shop and was minding her own business, stocking one of the displays, when the bells over the door chimed. She glanced over and spotted a tall blonde walking in. Her long hair was pulled back into a ponytail, and she was wearing black shiny pants, a white blouse, and black stilettos with four-inch heels. Ilsa blinked at her. The woman was very dressed up for Christmas Grove, especially that early in the morning. Still, Ilsa had the impression she'd seen her somewhere before. She just couldn't place her.

A young boy of about five or six ran into the store behind her. He skirted around her and practically flung himself against the plexiglass case that held most of the treats. "I need a chocolate croissant and two caramel clusters."

Lily smiled down at him. "Well, good morning to you, too."

Ilsa held back a snicker. Lily was no stranger to demanding little boys.

"Say good morning, Vin," his mother said.

"Good morning," he parroted.

"Now ask nicely for what you want," the woman said in a stern voice.

The child turned back to Lily and said, "Please, may I have a chocolate croissant and two caramel clusters?"

"Just one," his mother said.

"But, Mom, one is for me and one is for—"

"Your father. Right. Okay, get two." She tapped something out on her phone, and when she looked back up, she smiled warmly at Lily, who was handing her son the items he'd requested. "I'm going to need a Love Conquers All hot chocolate. Large and to-go."

Mrs. Pottson appeared from the back room. "I'll handle it, Lily." She gave the woman a tight smile and said, "Hello, Whitney. It's been a long time."

Whitney!

Zach's ex? What was she doing asking for a love potion?

"Oh, hello," Whitney said, giving Mrs. Pottson a forced smile. "It's nice to see you again."

Mrs. Pottson nodded to her and went about making her drink. "Is this for you or someone special in your life?"

"Does it really matter?" Whitney asked.

"Yes. If you want the proper potion it does." Mrs. Pottson's voice was tight, and if Ilsa wasn't mistaken, her boss didn't care for Whitney much.

"Fine. It's for someone else. We just need something to restart the flame if you know what I mean."

Mrs. Pottson nodded. "I see."

Ilsa's heart sped up as she thought about what Whitney could be alluding to. She'd been texting Zach that morning, and here she was in Christmas Grove. That couldn't be a coincidence, could it?

Mrs. Pottson handed Whitney the drink and rattled off her total.

Just as Whitney was paying for her purchases, her phone buzzed, and she muttered, "It's about time, Zach." Then she glanced at her son and said, "Let's go. Your father is waiting."

Ilsa's breath left her as she watched Whitney glide out the

door with her son in tow. Her entire body went numb as she asked Mrs. Pottson, "Zach has a son?"

Mrs. Pottson was glaring at the door when she said, "That's what it sounded like."

"No way," Lily said, her voice barely a whisper.

Ilsa let out a hysterical laugh. "He has a son. Of course he does. No wonder he's so good with Mia." She glanced at the clock. It was just past eight. He wasn't due to show up for another hour, but she couldn't wait. If she didn't get out of there, she was going to lose it. "Do you mind if I take a break? I could use some air."

"Take as long as you need," Mrs. Pottson said.

Ilsa nodded, took off her apron, and without even bothering to find her coat, she walked out of the shop into the chilly morning.

CHAPTER TWENTY-THREE

*Z*ach sat at his kitchen table with Mia in her carrier and a coffee mug in front of him as he stared at the string of text messages from Whitney. After the first one had come in, he'd ignored the rest. Instead, he'd come back to the house, showered and cleaned up, and then went to Holly's to pick up his daughter. Mia had been quite pleased to see him and had spent a fair amount of time making happy sounds at him before she'd fallen back to sleep.

After arming himself with coffee and a bagel, he'd finally turned his attention to his phone and then promptly wished he could block her. He would have if it weren't for Vin.

The texts were one after another, and they grew more and more manipulative in succession.

I miss you. You know how I get when we're not speaking. Please call me back before I do something I shouldn't.

Are you really going to just keep ignoring me? You can't ignore me forever. It's Christmas time. You'll be here for Christmas Eve, right? I already ordered your present. I think you're really going to like it. Not that there's much of it. She'd added a bikini emoji. Zach rolled his eyes and continued reading.

I'm seeing a therapist. She says I need to own my mistakes. All I want to do is apologize. You know you've always been the one for me. Don't throw away what we had over a little mistake.

I love you, and I'm sorry for what went down in March. I'm ready to make this work. You'll see.

He wasn't surprised that the texts had started at five o'clock. Zach had always been an early riser, and Whitney knew that. She also knew it was the best time to contact him during the holiday season, otherwise he'd be busy at the farm. He was surprised that she wanted to apologize. That was something she'd never tried before. But he'd never walked out and not returned before either.

The phone buzzed again.

Vin says he hasn't seen you in a few weeks. Don't you want to see him? He misses you.

Anger curled in his gut at her audacity to use Vin to try to worm her way back into his life. Zach hadn't seen Whitney since that day in March when he'd finally had enough and told her whatever had been between them was over. But he had visited Vin. He'd just chosen to see him when he was with his grandparents, which was every day after school while Whitney was at work. It was true that he hadn't made an effort to see Vin lately, but that had more to do with the farm than Ilsa or Mia. He just didn't have time in the afternoons. Whitney already knew that.

He tapped out a response. *Don't do that. Of course I want to see Vin. I just haven't had an afternoon off.*

Her reply was terse. *Well, at least you haven't abandoned him.*

Zach started to tap out another reply, but another text from her came in before he could finish.

Are you home?

Yes.

Good. We're on our way.

"On your way?" Zach said, frowning. Why wasn't Vin in school? What was she up to?

Mia let out a whimper, no doubt displeased at his outburst. He plucked her out of the carrier and tugged her to his chest. "Hey, sweetie. It's all right. Daddy didn't mean to wake you." She settled against him, and he walked around the house whispering to her until he felt her body relax into deep sleep. He took her and the baby carrier to the nursery and settled her into her crib. After kissing her forehead, he grabbed the baby monitor and went back into the kitchen and made more coffee. Clearly, he was going to need it.

The knock came too soon, and before he could even answer the door, it flew open. Vin rushed inside and made a beeline for Zach, wrapping his arms around him and burying his head into Zach's stomach.

"I missed you," Vin said, his voice muffled.

"I missed you, too." Zach mussed the kid's hair and then dropped to one knee so that he could give his favorite six-year-old a hug. "Looks like someone is playing hooky today. No school?"

"We have today off," Vin said. "So mom said I could come see you."

Zach glanced over at Whitney. She was leaning against the doorjamb in the kitchen, dressed as if she were going to a high-powered corporate job instead of the data entry position she'd started a few months ago. "And you? Are you off too?"

She shook her head. "I have about an hour before I have to be there." Whitney moved closer, holding out a cup from Love Potions. "I brought this for you."

He took it and eyed the cup suspiciously. "You didn't bring me a love potion, did you?"

"What?" she asked, pressing her palm to her chest. "That's a very rude thing to ask. As if I'd ever be so desperate that I'd resort to slipping you a love potion. Come on, Zach. You know me better than that."

He wanted to laugh. He did know her, and after six years of manipulation, he was quite certain she'd do just about anything to get her way.

"I got you something," Vin said, handing him a white paper bag.

Zach put the Love Potion drink on the table and took a peek in the bag. He pulled out the caramel cluster and grinned at Vin. "You're the man. Thank you."

Vin grinned up at him. "I knew you'd like it."

After popping the treat into his mouth, Zach ignored the Love Potions cup and grabbed the coffee he'd left on the table.

Whitney frowned. "What, you don't trust me now?"

Zach ignored the question and sat in a chair next to Vin. "Tell me what you've been up to."

Vin launched into a monologue about a game he and his friends had been playing. Zach made a point of listening and asking questions where appropriate. After a solid five minutes of in-depth details Zach was certain he'd never remember, Whitney cleared her throat.

"Vin, go play in the game room. I need to talk to Zach."

"Okay." Vin started to take off down the hall, but Zach caught hold of his hand, stopping him.

"Not in there, Vin." Zach said. He didn't want anyone waking up Mia. "Why don't you go out back and make a snowman before it melts?"

"Oh, yeah!" He ran off, and a few seconds later, they heard the door slam.

Immediately, Mia's cry came through the baby monitor, and Zach winced.

"What is that?" Whitney asked, glancing around with a horrified look on her face. "Is there a baby here?"

"Yes. There is a baby here," Zach said impatiently. "She was sleeping. Now if you'll excuse me, I need to see to my daughter."

"You have a daughter?" Whitney shrieked at the top of her lungs. "Since when? With who?"

Mia's cries were on a supersonic level after Whitney's outburst, and Zach let out a groan as he ignored Whitney's questions and hurried to the nursery. Mia's face was bright red and full of frustration.

"I know, sweetie. No one likes to be woken up in the middle of a nap. I know exactly how you feel." He scooped her up, quickly checked to make sure she was dry, and then carried her into the kitchen and grabbed the bottle he'd warmed just before she fell asleep. The moment she felt the tip of the bottle in her mouth, she wrapped her lips around it and started to suck.

"Thank the gods you shut her up," Whitney said.

Zach glared at her. "I think it's best if you leave now."

"I'm not leaving until you tell me what the hell is going on here," she said, placing her hands on her hips and glaring at him. "Because it looks like you were cheating on me."

A gasp came from the other side of the room.

Zach's eyes met Ilsa's wide ones. Her mouth was open in shock, and the blood had drained from her face.

Whitney whipped around and said, "Oh, is this the

homewrecker? She's not up to your usual standard, is she, Zach? I thought you only went for blondes."

"Whitney!" Zach admonished. "Shut up."

"Why? You don't want your little baby mama to know the truth?" Whitney's lips had curved into an evil grin. It was obvious she was enjoying torturing Ilsa.

"You're not speaking any kind of truth," Zach said. "Just go. Our conversation is over."

"Oh, it's far from over, sweetie," she said in that condescending tone he knew so well. "But since I have a real job, as opposed to one in some silly chocolate shop, I'm going. Try not to forget that your son is outside. I'll be by after work to pick him up."

Zach and Ilsa were silent as they both watched Whitney sweep out of the room and then slam the door behind her.

"Ilsa," Zach said. "I can explain."

She held her hand up, shook her head, and then turned on her heel and started to follow Whitney. But just as she reached the door, she turned around and walked back, taking up residence in the doorframe where Whitney had stood just minutes earlier. "Just tell me one thing."

"Anything," Zach said, his heart beating so hard against his chest he thought it might bruise his ribcage.

"Were you with her when we were together last Christmas?" she asked, her face pinched as if she really didn't want to know the answer.

"No. I swear to you, I wasn't."

Ilsa nodded and then visibly swallowed. "Is she the reason you ended things between us?"

"Yes. She called and said Vin needed me, so... I went." He hated that she'd been able to manipulate him so easily, but she knew his weakness was Vin, and she wasn't above using her own son to get whatever she wanted. It had taken him way too long to realize that fact.

"And that boy out there? He's your son?" she asked.

A lump got caught in his throat, and he swallowed hard before he finally forced out, "In all the ways that matter, yes."

CHAPTER TWENTY-FOUR

$\mathcal{I}$lsa slumped into one of the kitchen chairs, overwhelmed by what she'd walked in on. Zach had a son. She wasn't thrown because Vin existed; she was thrown because he'd never said anything about him. How had she known Zach almost her entire life, been best friends with Holly and Rex, and still hadn't known? Why was he hiding his child? He'd never hid Mia. Hadn't even attempted to deny her in any way. None of it made sense.

She glanced over at him and said, "I think you have a lot more explaining to do."

Zach ran both hands through his dark hair. "You're right. I do." He glanced at the clock on the wall. "Do you have time now? Or do you need to get back to work?"

Ilsa pulled out her phone and made a quick call to Love Potions. Before she could even explain that she needed the rest of the day off, Mrs. Pottson said, "No need to come back in. We've got the rest of the day covered. Just work out your issues with Zach. We'll see you tomorrow."

"You see visions, don't you?" Ilsa asked her.

"Something like that," Mrs. Pottson said. "And do yourself a favor and dump out that faux potion Whitney brought with her. It's useless and likely tastes like day old coffee by now."

Ilsa couldn't help but chuckle a little. Mrs. Pottson was meddlesome, but there was no denying that the woman was usually right on target. "I will. Thank you." After she ended the call, she got up, grabbed the cup, and poured the contents down the drain. She met Zach's eyes. "Mrs. Pottson made sure the potion was ineffective. You owe her a thank you."

"I will," he said, never taking his eyes off her.

Ilsa held her arms out to take Mia. Zach didn't hesitate as he handed her over. "Hi, baby girl. Mama missed you." Mia blinked up at her, her cheeks pink and her eyes bright.

"She's been sleeping most of the morning," Zach said.

"Until Whitney got here?" There was a sharpness to her tone that she didn't bother to try to hide.

"Vin slammed the door. That woke her up. Listen, Ilsa, I didn't know they were coming over today. Whitney just showed up with Vin in tow. I'd never have had them over without telling you about them."

"Exactly when were you going to tell me you have a son?" There was an ache in her stomach, but she ignored it, needing to hear his explanation. While every instinct told her to run, she couldn't do that. Zach was Mia's father, and she owed it to her daughter not to take off without at least listening. The hard truth was that she couldn't cut him out of Mia's life, so she was stuck trying to work things out, even if that meant just being civil for the sake of their daughter.

Zach leaned forward, held her gaze, and said, "When I got Whitney's text this morning, I decided I was going to tell you tonight."

Ilsa snorted. "Convenient."

"I suppose it looks that way." He sat back in his chair. "It's important to know that I wasn't hiding the fact that Vin exists. But there's more to the story, and it's not easy for me to talk about. In fact, I've never really told anyone the *whole* story. Not even Rex."

That got her attention. Although she was still hurt that she'd been left in the dark, she desperately wanted to know why this kind, open, and generous man had kept his secrets so close to the vest. "All right. I'm listening."

Zach got up, poured himself a fresh cup of coffee, and then sat back down. "Whitney and I dated for about a year before I learned she was pregnant. Back then, she was vibrant, full of life, and someone who was excellent at coaxing me out of my comfort zone. She was vivacious and brought fun into my life during a time that was especially trying."

Ilsa raised her eyebrows. "Was that around the time that you lost your brother?"

"Yes." Zach stared into his coffee. "Dane had just passed, and his wife and son moved back east to be near her parents, so not only was my brother gone, so was his family. We were close, and I had a hard time dealing with it. But Whitney... She was good at helping me live in the present. I fell in love with her because of it."

Hearing that he'd been in love with someone else wasn't an easy thing for Ilsa. The very idea of him being in love with the caustic woman who'd just stormed out of his house made her chest ache. But she just nodded, indicating that he should go on.

"I was away for about two months, working with a couple of other Christmas tree farms up north, and when I came home, Whitney sprang it on me that she was pregnant. I was understandably shocked and more than a little terrified, but I quickly adjusted to the news and was excited about starting a family. It's probably not a surprise that I've always wanted kids. It's no secret that family is important to me. So I went out and bought a ring, intending to ask Whitney to marry me."

Intending. He'd said intending. That meant it never happened. Some of the tension eased in her shoulders. "Why didn't you ask her?"

He let out a humorless chuckle. "My cousin Chris came to pay me a visit. He lives on the coast, so I was surprised he came all the way to Christmas Grove. It turned out that while I was away, he ended up spending time with Whitney." Zach took a long sip of coffee and glanced out the sunroom windows on the back of the house where Vin was playing with Spruce. "I actually met Whitney through him, so them socializing wasn't that unusual. They went to school together. I didn't even understand what the big deal was until he confessed that they'd been sleeping together the entire time I was away and that he was positive that the baby was his."

Ilsa gasped and quickly covered her mouth. Mia responded to the noise by letting out a loud squawk.

"Hey there, sweet Mia girl," Zach said quietly as he let her grab his finger with her hand for a moment before settling back in his seat.

"Vin isn't your biological son?" Ilsa asked in a hushed tone as she watched the happy little boy run around with Zach's Lab.

Zach shook his head. "Chris was right. He was the father. When I went to the doctor's appointment with her and found out the due date, it was clear there was no way I could be the baby's father. I left her then. Stopped talking to my cousin. Honestly, Ilsa, I went into a pretty dark place for a while. I didn't know what was going on with either of them, and then one day I got a call from Whitney. Chris overdosed one week before Vin was due."

Tears filled Ilsa's eyes, and she didn't bother to blink them back. He'd suffered through so much loss; it was heartbreaking. "I'm sorry, Zach. That must have been really hard."

He nodded. "Harder than you know. I was devastated. Even though he'd hurt me, I still loved him like my brother. I don't know how we could've moved past that rift, but I have to hold on to the idea that we could have."

Not knowing what to say, she reached out and squeezed his hand.

Zach turned his hand over and slipped his fingers through hers, entwining them. "I got a letter in the mail three days later. It was sent right before Chris died. He asked me to watch over his son as if he were my own."

Ilsa closed her eyes for a moment and tried to get herself under control. His story was heartbreaking. "The overdose wasn't an accident."

"No. It wasn't."

"Oh, Zach," she breathed, desperately wanting to get up and give him a hug. Just hold him and be a safe haven. But she knew he had more to say.

"It was maybe the second worst day of my life after losing my brother." Zach's eyes shone with unshed tears. "From that moment on, I was there for Whitney and Vin, standing in for Chris. Whitney and I got back together for a time. We were off and on for several years, but the relationship was just too volatile, and in March I finally walked away for good. The one thing that never changed is that I visit Vin every week. As I said before, I've been his father in all the ways that matter."

"Whitney doesn't seem to think it's over," Ilsa said and bit

DEANNA CHASE

her lip. She didn't want to come off as the jealous other woman, but she needed to know how things stood with Zach and Whitney if they were going to move forward.

"I don't see her." He shrugged. "Today is the first time I've seen her since March. Instead of going to her house, I visit him at his grandparents' house. They watch him after school while Whitney is at work."

"He never comes here?" She glanced around, wondering why. It was a great house, with trees as far as the eye could see.

He shook his head. "It takes over an hour to get from here to there. Whitney never wants to make the drive, and I was always willing. So I went there. He's been here a few times over the years, and he spent a couple of weekends here this summer, but that's it. Honestly, I'm shocked she brought him here today. But then maybe not. She's been trying to get me to head up to her house for over a week. I've been ignoring her."

"Maybe you should have told her about us. About Mia," Ilsa said, wondering why he'd kept the news to himself. Was he afraid of upsetting her?

Zach nodded. "I should have. No doubt about it. But I wanted to tell Vin first. He knows I'm not his biological dad, but that doesn't change the fact that I'm the only father he's ever known. I didn't want Whitney explaining it to him. She's... Well, she's developed a vindictive streak over the years. She's very unhappy when she doesn't get what she wants."

"That must be tough for both you and Vin," Ilsa said.

"For Vin. But not me. I'm over her. I was over her after I found out she cheated on me, but guilt and obligation kept me around." He brought her hand up to his lips and kissed it gently. "You have no idea how much I wish I'd have ignored her call last January. She said she wanted to go to therapy, to finally make things work, to put our family together for Vin.

192

And I…" He shook his head. "I love that little boy. I wanted to make it work for him. It was naïve to believe we could, though. Even with therapy, it was clear Whitney and I were never going to be compatible. She's more interested in reliving her twenties right now. She never wanted to move to Christmas Grove. Honestly, she was never interested in learning what I wanted out of life. It was all about her. I finally had enough."

"What is it that you want, Zach?" Ilsa asked, needing to hear him put it into words.

"You. Mia. More time with Vin." His dark gaze bored into her as he continued. "A life here on my farm. A family. Sleeping in on weekends. Breakfasts with Holly and Rex. A standing date with you at the Christmas Tree lighting in the square every year. Marriage. A couple more kids."

Ilsa's heart nearly beat out of her chest as it filled with a surge of love for the man sitting next to her. "That sounds wonderful."

"Does that mean you'd be interested in sharing a life like that with me?"

"Yes." Tears streamed down her face as she smiled at him. "You have no idea how long I've wanted to share that life with you."

Zach stood, tugged Ilsa to her feet, and wrapped his arms around both her and Mia. "I promise you and Mia can always count on me. I won't walk away again. Count on it."

She stared up at him, her insides bursting with love for the man who held her. "And I promise to always communicate with you even when it's hard. I'll be here, right by your side, no matter what."

Zach let out a breath, one that she guessed he'd been figuratively holding ever since she'd walked in on him and Whitney. "I love you, Ilsa."

There was no stopping the tears as she said, "I love you, too, Zach."

The pair had just broken apart when the back door opened, and Vin and Spruce ran into the house.

"Dad! I taught Spruce a new trick," Vin said excitedly, his face bright and full of joy.

"You did?" Still holding one of Ilsa's hands, Zach crouched down to talk to Vin on his level. "Let's see it."

Vin clapped his hands and let out a barely audible whistle.

Spruce stopped spinning in circles and gave the boy his full attention.

Laughing, Vin said, "Good boy." Then Vin started to shuffle his feet from side to side and added, "Dance, Spruce."

The dog mimicked Vin's movements... sort of. His tail was going a million miles an hour while he tapped his feet and his head bobbed in time with Vin's rhythm.

"Wow, Vin. That's really something. You and Spruce could be the next YouTube sensations," Zach said.

"You think?" His eyes went wide, and he bounced on the balls of his feet. "We have to video it. I'll get my phone."

"Hold on a minute. I want you to meet some people." Zach smiled up at Ilsa, who was still holding his daughter. "It's time you met your little sister, Mia."

The boy went perfectly still as he stared at the baby in Ilsa's arms. "Sis... sister?"

Zach nodded. "Yes. Mia is your little sister. I'm hoping you'll get to spend lots of time with her."

Vin glanced from Mia to Zach and then up at Ilsa. "Are you her mom?"

Ilsa nodded. "I sure am. My name is Ilsa. It's really nice to meet you, Vin."

He frowned, and his face scrunched up in confusion. "Are you my dad's girlfriend?"

Ilsa glanced over at Zach. He gave her a reassuring smile that prompted her to say, "Yes, I am."

Vin nodded. "Cool. I've always wanted a sister." As soon as the words were out of his mouth, the boy ran into the living room and then immediately returned with an older model iPhone.

Ilsa raised a questioning eyebrow. He was pretty young to have a phone, wasn't he?

Zach seemed to read her mind, because he leaned in and whispered, "I gave him my old one so I could always reach him. It's full of parental controls. No need to worry, Mom."

Ilsa rolled her eyes at him. "What do I know? I'm new at this."

Zach gave her a kiss on her cheek and said, "Don't worry. I'll teach you."

And as she watched him interact with Vin, she had no doubt he would.

CHAPTER TWENTY-FIVE

"Can I ask you something?" Ilsa turned to face Zach. They were sitting on a bench in front of his office, watching as Rex gave Vin a piggyback ride around the Christmas tree farm. Holly was sitting nearby with Mia, playing peek-a-boo with her.

"Sure." He turned into her, twining his fingers around hers. He'd barely let go of her hand since she'd told him she loved him. It was like a physical need to keep touching her.

"How come most people don't know about Vin? I assume Rex did, but I've never heard him or Holly talk about him."

It was a fair question. "I haven't been hiding him." Zach waved a hand at Vin, indicating that he had no problem with anyone at the farm seeing him there. "It's just that right around the time he was born, I knew he wasn't mine, right? And then when I started helping Whitney take care of him, it wasn't as if we were telling him I was his dad. That discussion came later. Much later, actually, when he asked if I was his dad. Whitney and I were together then, so she just shrugged and said, 'I guess so.' I explained I wasn't his biological dad, which I'm sure he didn't understand at the time, and then told him I'd be honored to be his dad if he wanted me to be. That was that. From that time on, he's always called me dad."

"That's a tricky situation," Ilsa said.

"You can say that again." He still remembered how nervous he was when Vin had asked that question and how elated he'd been when Vin had been thrilled to call him dad. "So even though I've always loved him like he's my son, it was a gradual process getting there. And since I was always going to Whitney's to visit him, it just really never came up here. And before you ask, I don't think Holly knows the story. Rex does, but his opinion of Whitney is pretty low, so it's not something he talks about. Not even to me, except when he told me to get my head out of my ass when it came to you."

It was Ilsa's turn to laugh. "When was that?"

"Last year after our first date. He basically told me I was crazy if I let you go."

"He was right." Ilsa nodded toward Rex, who had just glanced over at them. He waved back and continued to cart Vin around the lot as he talked to a family looking for a tree.

"No kidding. I've decided to seek his advice for all life decisions. I wonder what he'll say if I ask him when we should start trying for another child."

Ilsa jerked around to stare at him in horror. "Seriously? I just had that one."

He threw his head back and laughed. "Maybe I'll stick to just seeking your counsel."

"Good plan. But just because I'm not ready to *try* for another, that doesn't mean I don't want a lot of practice. Understood?"

"Perfectly," he said, his tone husky.

Ilsa leaned in and kissed him.

"Where's my child? I thought you were watching him." The chilly voice of none other than Whitney caused Ilsa to jerk away from Zach.

Zach waved a hand toward Rex. "He's right there, Whit."

The ice queen, as Ilsa had come to think of her, narrowed her eyes at Zach. "Go get my child. I need to get on the road."

Sighing, Zach squeezed Ilsa's hand and then climbed down the porch and made his way over to Rex.

Ilsa cleared her throat. "Did you have a good day at work?"

"No. By the time I got there, half the morning was gone. And I had to leave early just so that Vin and I can get home in time to meet my boss for drinks later. I'll be playing catch-up all day tomorrow." She placed her hands on her hips and started tapping a foot, clearly impatient that Zach wasn't moving faster.

"We could've watched him. I'm sure Zach would've been fine bringing him home later tonight or tomorrow," Ilsa said. "He's such a lovely child. We really enjoyed—"

"Who do you think you are?" Whitney hissed, turning on her. "Whatever this is between you and Zach, it won't last. Mark my words, in another month, he'll be back on my doorstep."

"I doubt it," Ilsa said, her tone as cold as Whitney's.

The tall blonde laughed. "Zach's been in love with me for years. That doesn't just go away. So enjoy your little fling, but know that just like last time, he'll leave you and come home where he belongs."

"Home?" Ilsa scoffed. "You think your house is home?" She shook her head. "You really don't know him at all, do you?"

"I know what he sounds like when I satisfy him in my bed. I think that's plenty of knowledge." Her shit-eating grin just made Ilsa roll her eyes.

"Classy," she muttered.

"Listen, you little tramp," Whitney said, her tone low and full of warning. "Zach is mine. He always has been, and he always will be. Don't make the mistake of thinking he can just walk away from me. We share things you have no clue about. When I call, he'll come running."

"If you say so," Ilsa said, wondering how Zach had put up with her for so long. Then her gaze landed on the sweet little boy who'd climbed on Zach's back and was laughing as Zach bounced him up and down. That right there was the reason. Not Whitney.

Whitney glanced over to see what Ilsa was looking at, and understanding flashed in her pale eyes. "If you try to keep him from me, I'll keep Vin from him. His time as Dad will be over."

Ilsa stared at the woman, completely horrified that she'd use her child as a pawn in order to control Zach. Though she supposed Whitney had already been doing that for years in order to get what she wanted out of Zach. "You'd punish your own child just to get your way?"

Whitney hesitated as she eyed her son with Zach. Instead of answering, she said, "Zach isn't his real dad. Did he tell you that?"

"Yes. But that doesn't change the way your son feels about him."

The other woman visibly flinched, and Ilsa knew she'd hit the right nerve.

"You aren't going to keep Vin from him," Ilsa said with an air of authority.

"Who do you think you are, telling me what I'm going to do?" Whitney sneered at her. "Who are you, anyway? Just a baby mama who went and got herself knocked up. Now what?

You think he's going to marry you? Well, I have news for you, he's not the marrying type. Trust me. I know."

Ilsa wanted to laugh. Zach *was* the marrying type. That much was clear. He just wasn't going to marry someone he didn't trust and who didn't want the type of life he did. Ilsa knew the other woman was just trying to get a rise out of her. She wouldn't give Whitney the satisfaction. "You won't keep Vin from Zach because you love your son. You might threaten Zach to try to get your way, but we both know in the end that you love your son more than you want to punish Zach for walking away after years of a rocky relationship."

The two women stared each other down until Zach and Vin were right in front of them.

Zach cleared his throat. "Is everything all right here?"

Whitney turned her steely gaze on him. "It's perfect. Vin, say goodbye to your dad. We're leaving."

Zach hugged Vin, told him to call when they got home, and then stood back and watched them walk away. "What just happened here?"

Ilsa smiled up at him. "Nothing to worry about." She stood and wrapped her arm around him. "Whitney and I just came to an understanding, that's all."

He let out a nervous laugh. "Do I even want to know?"

"Probably not." She pressed up on her tiptoes and whispered in his ear. "Holly's on baby duty for the next hour. How about we ditch the farm and head back to your place. I was thinking about testing out that double-headed shower of yours."

His lips curved into a slow grin. "Lead the way."

CHAPTER TWENTY-SIX

*S*haring his home with Ilsa and Mia was everything Zach had thought it would be. He adored waking up next to the woman he loved and tucking his child in at night. He didn't even mind getting up in the middle of the night to care for Mia. In fact, he sort of lived for those moments in the quiet night when it was just the two of them while the rest of the world slumbered.

Between the traffic at the farm, taking care of Mia, and making up for lost time with Ilsa in the bedroom department, he wasn't getting quite enough sleep, but he wouldn't have it any other way. And that's why he was dead to the world on his couch when a loud knocking on his door jolted him awake. "Hold on!" he croaked.

Zach opened the door to find Rex standing on his porch holding a thick envelope. "Where's the fire?"

"Were you sleeping?" Rex glanced at the clock. "It's two in the afternoon."

"I know. I was napping. We've got a baby in this house." He rubbed at his eyes. "What did you need?" He turned and walked through the house to the kitchen, intent on making a fresh pot of coffee. "Is something up at the farm?"

"No." Rex slapped the envelope on the counter. "This came certified mail for Ilsa. I figured it must be important."

Zach picked up the envelope. The return address was from a law firm in San Rafael, California. Dread coiled in his gut. Hadn't Ilsa said her ex was a lawyer from the Bay Area?

"Bad news?" Rex asked.

"I think so." Zach left Rex in the kitchen and walked down the hallway to the nursery where he found Ilsa sound asleep in the rocker and Mia in the crib. He crouched down in front of Ilsa and ran his hands lightly up her arms. "Hey, sleepyhead. Time to wake up."

Ilsa's eyes fluttered open. She blinked a few times before focusing on him. "Is it almost time to leave for the Christmas Ball?"

Every year the town put on a Christmas Ball in the square, and they had plans to go. "No. It's just after two o'clock. Rex brought a letter by. I think it might be important."

Ilsa let out a big yawn and stretched her arms over her head. "I'm not expecting any letters. Who's it from?"

"A law firm in the Bay Area. Richards, Baylor, and Sparta. Ring a bell?"

"Oh, hell." She shot to her feet. "I thought Kevin had given up bothering me." She hurried out of the room, and after checking Mia once more, Zach followed his girlfriend into the kitchen.

Ilsa stood at the counter, shaking with the letter in her hand.

"What does it say?" Zach asked, gently taking the letter from her.

"It's a custody hearing. Kevin is trying to get partial

custody." She shook her head in disbelief. "How can he do that? He's not her father. I don't get it."

Zach scanned the letter and confirmed that Kevin was indeed forcing her to court for a custody battle. He also couldn't believe the man had decided to pursue the courts when he hadn't even asked for a paternity test. Not that it would do him any good. Anger pumped through Zach's veins. The guy couldn't possibly want anything to do with Mia. This was a ploy to mess with Ilsa. He was sure of it. "I don't know why he's doing this, Ilsa." Zach kissed the top of her head. "But we have facts and the law on our side. Let me call Effie and see what we need to do."

"Effie?" Ilsa asked.

"My lawyer. After the last time Kevin showed up, I told her this might be a possibility and forwarded the results of my paternity test. Remember that she called both of us and said with that test and the lack of his name on the birth certificate, he has zero case. So try not to worry too much about this. The case will likely be dismissed."

"Likely?" she squeaked. "I don't remember her using the word *likely*!"

Zach wrapped his arms around her and pulled her into a hug. "Very likely. He's not Mia's dad. No court is going to give him partial custody."

She pressed her face into his shoulder and muttered, "I hate that jackass. What was I thinking?"

Zach chuckled softly. "I ask myself that every time I have to deal with Whitney. Let's just call them starter relationships. You know, the ones that show us exactly what we *don't* want."

She pulled back and looked up at him. "They were both harsh lessons."

"I agree completely." He leaned in and kissed her.

Rex cleared his throat.

Zach looked over Ilsa's head at his friend. "What's up?"

"I hate to be the bearer of bad news, but Whitney just pulled up outside."

"Whitney? What the hell is she doing here?" Zach let go of Ilsa and stalked to the front door, opening it and finding Whitney poised to knock. "Whitney, what's going on?"

She dropped her hand and pushed Vin forward. "My boss is taking me out of town until after New Year's. Vin wanted to stay here with you instead of with his grandparents." She waved at her car, where Vin was trying to wrestle a suitcase out of the back seat. "I figured you wouldn't say no."

Zach frowned at her. "You couldn't have called to give us some warning?"

"Us?" Whitney asked, her entire body going rigid with anger. "Are you telling me you need to clear this with your baby mama now?"

Sighing, Zach shook his head. "I'm sure Ilsa will be fine with it. I just meant... You know what? Never mind. Yes, I'm thrilled to have him here for the holidays. Go enjoy your... work trip." He didn't believe for a second the trip had anything to do with work. It might have been with her boss; that part was debatable. But he was certain there was no reason for someone in data entry to be traveling over the holidays.

She gave him a tight smile before turning around and walking to her car. When she reached Vin, she yanked out his suitcase, gave him a hug and a kiss, and then jumped in the car and sped down the drive.

Right at that moment, Spruce bolted from the trees and rammed right into Vin, knocking him down into the mud. The boy let out a squeal of delight as Spruce licked every inch of his face.

"Well, this is a surprise," Ilsa said from behind him.

He turned and gave her an apologetic smile. "I'm sorry. I had no idea he was coming."

Ilsa patted his arm. "I know. But don't be sorry. I like having Vin around. He's a cool kid."

"He'd be cooler if he wasn't covered in mud," Zach said.

"At least he'll have good skin," Ilsa joked.

Rex joined them on the porch, holding a red-faced Mia. His tone was a little desperate when he asked, "Is this what it's like all the time when you have kids?"

"Yes," Ilsa and Zach said at the same time.

"That's what I was afraid of." Grimacing, he handed Mia to Zach and took off through the trees back toward Holly's house.

"I think someone is a little freaked out," Ilsa said.

"A little is an understatement." Zach eyed Vin and shook his head. The kid was covered from head to toe with mud. "Hey, Vin," he called. "Bring Spruce and get in here. You need a bath before we go out."

"Out where?" he called back without diverting his attention from Spruce, who was trying to dig a hole at his feet.

"To Ilsa's parents' house. There's going to be hot chocolate and fresh cookies," he said, hoping they didn't mind having an extra kid for the evening. Otherwise, he'd have to drop Ilsa off so she could work the Love Potions booth at the ball, and he'd stay home and take care of the kids.

"Okay." Vin snapped his fingers and said, "Let's go, Spruce." The dog fell into step beside him, and then both of them tracked mud all the way through the house to the hallway bathroom.

They both stared at the muddy footprints.

"I need to call the lawyer," Zach said, just as Ilsa said, "I need to feed Mia."

Zach glanced down at his daughter. She was smiling and relatively quiet. "I think you have me confused with someone who doesn't know you're just trying to get out of cleaning mud off our hardwood floors."

Ilsa let out a laugh, rolled her eyes, and added, "Fine. I'll clean the floors. You take care of the boy and his dog. After the phone call to the lawyer."

"On it." Zach swept into the house, careful to avoid the mud, and went straight for his phone. When he heard the older woman answer the phone, he said, "Effie we have a problem."

The lawyer made a snapping sound with her gum and said, "Lay it on me."

CHAPTER TWENTY-SEVEN

"*T*ry to relax, okay?" Zach said, holding Ilsa's hand as he guided her through the crowd in the square. The annual Christmas Ball festivities were well underway. Twirling snowmen were putting on a show on the dancefloor, while animated reindeer were jumping and playing in a roped off area, one with a distinct red nose. Perpetual snowflakes hung in the air, and there were faerie lights everywhere, illuminating the square. The tree, a giant one from Zach's farm, stood in the middle, towering over everyone.

"I'm trying," she said, but all she really wanted to do after receiving the letter from Kevin's lawyer was to stay home and hold Mia. And that's exactly what she would have done if Mrs. Pottson hadn't been counting on her to help at the booth where they were selling holiday cheer potions and hot chocolate. Instead, her mother was watching Mia and Vin. The little boy hadn't been too pleased with the arrangement until he found out her mother had a heated pool that they kept open year-round. It was her mom's water witch abilities that made it possible in an area that saw snow semi-regularly through the winter months.

"Effie has it under control. I promise," he said for the third time in under an hour.

Ilsa wished she had his confidence, but the custody case didn't make any sense. Kevin didn't want to be a father. Of that she was certain. It felt more like he was just trying to terrorize her. Either way, she wished she'd never met the bastard.

Zach led her over to the Love Potions booth and gave her a kiss on the cheek. "I'll meet you back here in an hour, all right?"

"Yeah, that should be fine." She wrapped her arms around him and said, "Thank you for calling Effie. It does make me feel better, I just..." Ilsa sighed, not sure what else to say.

"I know, babe. It'll be fine. We both know he has no rights here."

She nodded. "I know. I just want it to be over."

"It will be." He kissed her temple and waited for her to take her place inside the booth before waving and walking off to find Holly and Rex.

"Hey, you," Lily said, giving her a smile. "Merry Christmas Ball."

Ilsa chuckled and scanned the other woman, admiring her formfitting, green velvet dress and Mary Jane-style heels. "You look lovely."

"So do you. That dress is gorgeous."

The black dress had a corset top and a black velvet skirt on the bottom. Ilsa had pared it with a short-waisted velvet jacket, and when she'd first tried it on, she'd felt beautiful and feminine for the first time in months. Motherhood was hard on the body, and the dress had stuffed all her parts back where they were supposed to go. "Thank you. It feels good to get dressed up again."

Lily laughed. "No kidding. When I'm not working, it's yoga pants and T-shirts. I usually just feel lucky if I'm not running around with a stain on my shirt."

The two laughed about motherhood in between helping customers with their drinks, and to Ilsa's surprise, the hour went by in a blink of an eye.

"Hello ladies," a familiar voice said from behind them in the tent.

Ilsa turned around and spotted Chase Garland, the chocolatier who worked with them at Love Potions. He was dressed in a well-tailored suit that showed off his broad shoulders, and he had a five o'clock shadow that made him look more 007 than chocolatier. "Wow," Ilsa said. "You clean up nice."

"So do you." Chase turned his attention to Lily and smiled at her. "Good evening, Lily. You're looking lovely this evening."

"Uh... um, yeah," she said, apparently unable to form a coherent reply.

Ilsa chuckled to herself.

Lily sent her a panicked look.

"Chase, do you think you could grab another sleeve of cups?" Ilsa said, pointing to the supplies behind the tent. "If it gets busy again, you guys will need them."

"Sure."

The moment he was out of sight, Ilsa grabbed Lily in a hug and whispered, "Just relax. He might be drop dead gorgeous in that suit, but remember, so are you. No need to be nervous. He'd be lucky to have a chance with you."

Lily stepped back from her embrace and glanced around

quickly before saying, "I'm not interested in Chase. That's not... He just surprised me is all."

Ilsa laughed. "Sure you're not." Then she winked, grabbed her jacket, and waved to Chase as he returned with the cups. "You two have a great evening. I'm going to find Zach so he can spin me around the dancefloor before we head home."

The pair waved at her, and Ilsa didn't miss the way Lily was standing awkwardly next to Chase, clearly trying to look anywhere else. That was going to be an interesting dynamic to watch at work over the next few weeks, Ilsa thought. At least it would give her something to distract herself with while she waited for news from the court about the custody hearing.

Ilsa paused at the end of food row where there were less people and glanced at her phone, noting that Zach was fifteen minutes late. He'd said he'd meet her at the tent in an hour, but it was well past that now. She sent him a text to find out where he was, and then waited. And waited. And waited some more.

"Where the heck is he?" she muttered and sent Holly a text.

Her friend messaged back instantly. *He went to find you about ten minutes ago. You haven't seen him?*

After texting Holly back, Ilsa turned around, intending to double back to the Love Potions tent, certain that they'd just missed each other. She'd only taken a few steps when a hand wrapped around her wrist, stopping her. A smile curled her lips as she turned back around, expecting to see Zach. But then she froze when she stared into the cool gray eyes of Kevin Loman.

Ilsa yanked her wrist out of his grasp. "What are you doing here?"

"I came to get what's mine." There was a chill in his gaze that shifted to heat as he scanned her body. "You're looking really good tonight, Ilsa. I'm glad to see it. No one wants a girlfriend who lets herself go."

She gaped at him. "What did you just say?"

"You heard me. Once we get you and Mia home, I'll hire you a personal trainer. Your curves look great, but you could use some toning before I start to show you off at the office parties."

The man was a caricature of pure evil. Again, she wondered how she had ever dated the jackass standing in front of her. "You're delusional if you think either of us are going anywhere with you. Mia isn't yours, and Zach and I can prove it. So back the hell off, Kevin. You have no business here." Ilsa felt the tremor in her voice and prayed that he hadn't heard it.

His lips curved into a small, cold smile. "I don't think your precious Zach is going to care about you when he finds out you've run off with your ex." He grabbed her wrist again, and this time, he twisted her arm so that he was holding it at an angle behind her back.

"Ouch! Let go!" she cried, glancing around, hoping someone would hear her. But the festivities were loud, and the area they were in seemed to suddenly be deserted.

"No." He pressed himself to her back, and she felt his hot breath as he whispered in her ear. "You're coming with me. We're going to go get our daughter and then we're going home. Christmas Grove isn't good for you, Ilsa. Can't you see that?"

This was not happening. No way was she going anywhere with that lunatic. And she'd go down fighting if she had to. She'd taken some basic self-defense classes when she was a teenager, and some of the old moves she'd studied kicked in. She quickly stomped on his foot and brought her free elbow up, knocking him in the face.

"Ouch! Son of a bitch!" he cried as he let go of her.

Ilsa took off running into the crowd, her heart racing and adrenaline pumping through her. She had to find Zach or the town sheriff, but she had no idea where either would be, and she wasn't stopping to use her phone. Not yet.

A dancing snowman got in her way, and Ilsa quickly dodged him but then managed to collide with someone in a cloud of yellow. They went down with an oomph, and the other woman started cursing up a storm before she finally stopped and stared right at Ilsa.

"Ilsa McKenzie! What in the world are you doing, trying to kill me?" Lemon Pepperson admonished. She stared down at her dress and cursed again. "Now there's a chocolate stain on my skirt."

Ilsa squinted at the woman's attire. The dress was miles and miles of bright yellow chiffon that was puffed out in layers of fabric. It looked like the dress had swallowed her up, leaving only her head and legs from the knees down showing. Ilsa got to her feet and offered the other woman a hand. "Sorry about that."

"You're going to pay for this," she hissed.

"No doubt."

"Ilsa, dammit!" Kevin's voice rang in her ears. "Do you think you can assault me and get away with it?"

She spun around and ducked just as Kevin's hand came out to grasp her around the neck. His momentum propelled him forward, unable to stop his motion. And for a second time, Lemon Pepperson went down in a heap, this time with Kevin on top of her.

"You dumb piece of reindeer poop. Get the hell off me." Lemon flailed beneath him, kicking and screaming.

"Shut up," Kevin demanded and grabbed both of her wrists, pinning her down.

Ilsa, who had jerked forward, intending to grab Kevin to knock him off of Lemon, was held back by a strong arm just as Lemon found purchase and kneed Kevin in the balls.

Kevin let out a grunt, fell over, and curled into himself as Lemon scrambled to her feet. "Bastard," she said and then spit on him.

Ilsa struggled to get away from her second attacker but then stilled when she heard Zach's calming voice.

"It's me, Ilsa. It's okay. It's just me," he wrapped his arms around her from behind, holding her close.

She twisted in his arms and buried her face in his shoulder. "Someone needs to get the sheriff," she said, her voice muffled. "He tried to force me to go with him."

"Shh, sweetheart. He's already here." Zach gently released her and turned her around so that she could see a tall, dark-haired man in a uniform kneeling down on the ground, already cuffing Kevin's hands behind his back.

"Well, well, well. Who do we have here?" A woman with long silver hair wearing a red Christmas sweater and a skirt made of green taffeta asked as she walked up to them.

"Effie, hi." Zach held his hand out to the lawyer who was working on their case.

"Where did you come from?" Ilsa asked, confused. "How did you know Kevin was here?"

"I didn't. I saw the commotion from over there." She waved toward the bar area where men dressed in tuxes were handing out champagne. "When I saw you and Zach, I figured you might need my help."

Ilsa let out a sigh of relief. "That's Kevin. He just tried to force me to go home with him. He grabbed me and twisted my arm behind my back until I elbowed him in the face and got away. Then he tried to attack me again and got Lemon instead. She quite literally kicked him in the balls."

Effie laughed. "I can't think of a better punishment for that..." She pressed her lips together and then said, "Soon-to-be-ex lawyer."

"I didn't do anything!" Kevin cried. The sheriff had already gotten him on his feet and was asking Lemon questions. "My license isn't in danger."

"It will be when the court finds out you falsified a notice for a court hearing," she said with ice in her tone. "There's no record of a custody hearing. Which makes sense since you have zero grounds for custody. I'll be filing a report first thing in the morning."

Kevin's eyes nearly popped out of his head. "You can't do that! The court hearing is valid. There must just be a recording error."

Effie shrugged. "Maybe. Maybe not. But when they find out you assaulted two women here tonight, that's not going to help you. Good luck, Mr. Loman." Effie squeezed Ilsa's shoulder. "The sheriff will probably want a statement. Do you want me to go with you?"

Ilsa nodded, just because the woman's presence had a calming effect on her. "Is it true? Is the custody hearing notice a fake?"

She nodded. "Completely. It's not only fake, it's a sloppy one, too. He did it to scare you. It's very likely he'll lose his license. And if his firm is reputable, he'll certainly lose his job since he used their letterhead." Effie glanced at him. "Not very bright, is he?"

Ilsa shook her head, leaned into Zach, and let out a sigh of relief. As long as there was no court hearing and Mia wasn't in any danger of being under Kevin's control, she could deal with the rest. She glanced up at Zach. "Let's go. I want my statement on the record." She turned to Effie. "Can I file a restraining order?"

Effie smiled at her. "I already started the paperwork this afternoon."

CHAPTER TWENTY-EIGHT

"*Merry* Christmas!" Ilsa called as she and her budding family walked in the back door of Holly and Rex's house. The scent of sugar and chocolate filled the air, and there was Christmas music playing in the background.

"Give me that little munchkin!" Holly cried as she came striding into the kitchen. "Oh, my stars. This is the cutest thing I've ever seen." She took Mia out of her baby carrier and held her up so everyone could see her reindeer costume. "Are you helping Santa deliver his packages tonight?"

Vin, who was right behind Ilsa, scoffed. "She's too little to help Santa."

Zach chuckled. "You're probably right, buddy. Go in the living room and say hello to your uncle Rex."

"Grab a cookie for both of you on the way," Holly called after him.

Vin rushed over to the cookie tray sitting in the middle of the table, grabbed two in the shape of Christmas trees, and ran off to find Rex.

Zach gave Holly a kiss on the cheek and then took the presents they'd brought and followed Vin into the next room.

"You look amazing," Ilsa told Holly as she put the baby carrier down and went to pour her and Zach mugs of hot cocoa that was warming on the stove. "Are you using a new moisturizer or something? I don't think I've ever seen your skin glow like that before."

Holly flushed a pretty shade of pink. "No. But I have started taking extra vitamins."

Ilsa, who'd been about to take a sip of her hot cocoa, put the mug down on the counter and moved over to stand in front of her friend. "It's happening, isn't it?" Her breath caught as she added, "Are you just trying, or are you pregnant?"

"Six weeks," Holly whispered.

"Ohmigod!" Ilsa cried and wrapped her arms around her friend, who was still holding Mia. "I'm so excited for you. Our babies are going to grow up together."

"I guess that means the cat is out of the bag," Rex said, standing in the doorway.

"Oops." Holly, who was still holding onto Ilsa, sent him a wide smile. "She sort of guessed."

"I'm sure." He chuckled and held his hands up in a surrender motion. "I knew there was no keeping it a secret from you two."

"Congratulations, man," Zach said, clasping him on the back. "Welcome to fatherhood. It's exhausting."

They all laughed and moved into the living room where they opened presents, drank too much cocoa, ate far too many cookies, and reveled in the holiday cheer. It was the perfect evening with close friends before they all went over to Ilsa's mother's house in the morning for the family gathering.

When all the wrapping paper had been cleared and the

cookie plate decimated, Zach got up and went to stand next to the tree. He held his hand out to Ilsa, indicating she should join him.

She laughed nervously. "Um, what's going on?"

Zach pushed a lock of her dark hair behind her ear and smiled down at her. "Ilsa McKenzie, it's been a wild month."

She glanced at Mia, who was in her carrier again, sleeping, and then at Vin who was busy playing with a set of Legos they'd given him. "Yes, you can definitely say that again."

"I wish I was saying it's been a wild year. We lost a lot of time being stubborn and not communicating. And worse, being afraid of the future."

Ilsa's eyes began to sting from unshed tears. She gave him a wobbly smile as she whispered, "What are you doing, Zach?"

His smile widened as he reached into his pocket, pulled out a red velvet box and then sank onto one knee.

"What?" Ilsa glanced wildly around the room, taking in the beaming faces of Holly and Rex. Something about the way they were watching her told her they'd known this was coming. Tears started to stream down her face unchecked as she focused on Zach. "Is this really happening?"

He nodded and opened the box, revealing a modest-size princess cut diamond. "It took me a long time to figure out what I needed in my life to feel whole. And even longer to realize who I wanted to share this life with. But now that I have, there's no doubt in my mind that I want to spend every day of the rest of my life with you, Ilsa McKenzie. Would you marry me and do me the honor of being my wife and the mother of our children and any more we're blessed with?"

The lump in her throat rendered her speechless. Her heart was swollen with so much love she was afraid it was going to burst. "Yes," she finally forced out, the words barely audible.

She cleared her throat and again said, "Yes. A million times, yes."

Zach's face was wet with tears as he slipped the ring on her finger and then rose to take her into his arms. "I love you so much, Ilsa."

"I love you, too," she said, clinging to him. "So much. But you know what this means, right?"

"What's that?"

"I'm never going to hear the end of this from my mother. Just imagine what she's going to say when we tell her we're getting married," Ilsa said with a half sob-half laugh.

Zach just smiled. "I guess we'll have to give her this one, huh? Maybe sometimes moms really do know best... even if she overstepped a bit."

"A bit!" Ilsa shook her head. "You're too generous. But I guess you're right. We'll just have to give her this one."

Vin appeared at their side, staring up at them. "Is Ilsa going to be my new mom?"

Ilsa's heart nearly broke in half at the confused look on the little boy's face.

Zach kneeled down and took his son in his arms. "Remember what I told you earlier today?"

Vin nodded. "That no matter what, you'll always be my dad and my mom will always be my mom."

"And about Ilsa?" he prompted.

"That she loves both of us, and there's always room for more love."

Oh goodness. Ilsa really was going to die from her heart exploding.

"That's right. She'll be your stepmom if you want her to be. Or she can just be Ilsa, dad's wife who loves and cares for you very much."

Ilsa couldn't stay silent. She placed a soft hand on Vin's shoulder and said, "Your dad's right. I love you. Your dad loves you. And your mom loves you, too. That's all that really matters, buddy. The rest can be decided later."

He beamed up at her. "I'm glad my dad is marrying you. You make him smile."

Ilsa wrapped the child into her arms and gave him a long hug. "Thank you, Vin. That means the world to me."

"Oh, man. I may never stop crying," Holly said, leaning into Rex.

"The bride and groom!" Rex said, producing a bottle from somewhere that looked like champagne.

Holly lined up four flutes and a plastic cup for Vin. "Sparkling cider," she said, winking at Ilsa. "We needed something celebratory that we could all have."

Ilsa stared at her friend. "How did you manage to keep all of this to yourself?" She shook her head. "I would've died trying to keep my mouth shut. First your pregnancy and now this?" She patted Zach's chest, so happy she thought she'd explode into a thousand pieces of confetti. When she thought back to the past year and how anxious she'd been about being a single mom and finally coming clean with Zach, she just felt foolish. But she was done worrying about what might have been, and was ready to live in the now and be grateful for all her blessings.

"Zach only told us earlier today about his plans, and I've only known about the pregnancy for a few days." She smiled shyly at Rex. "We were going to wait until after Christmas to tell everyone. But then we made plans for New Year's Eve, so I hope you didn't have anything too special planned." Her gaze landed on Rex, her eyes still glistening with tears.

He gently wiped them away before turning to their friends.

"We set the date. New Year's Eve, right here in the Christmas tent."

"Seriously?" Ilsa asked, taken aback. "This New Year's Eve? As in seven days from now?"

Holly nodded. "I'm not going to decorate. The tent is already magical. It'll just be a simple wedding with our closest friends."

"Holly and I would very much like it if you both would be our maid of honor and best man," Rex said.

"Of course," Ilsa and Zach said at the same time, making their friends laugh.

"It appears we have many blessings to celebrate tonight," Zach said, handing a flute to each of the adults and the plastic cup to Vin. When they were all holding their drinks up, he said, "To a life filled with love, friendship, and family."

They all echoed his toast, sipped the cider, and then spent the rest of the night making plans for the future.

CHAPTER TWENTY-NINE
ELEVEN MONTHS LATER

*L*ily Paddington stared at the too-handsome-for-his-own-good man sitting next to her in the shiny red SUV. Chase Garland was a tall man with wavy blond hair, wide shoulders, and a five o'clock shadow that never seemed to quit. From the moment she'd mentioned that she liked it the year before at the Christmas Ball, he'd kept it, as if her compliment had been the catalyst in convincing him of his new look.

And it drove her insane. She couldn't count how many times she'd wanted to reach out and caress his jawline, to feel that stubble under her touch. But that night at the Christmas Ball when they'd been dancing kept flashing in her mind, splashing a cold dash of reality over her daydreams. It had been just before midnight. The enchanted snow was falling, and the stars were twinkling bright. Chase had been a perfect gentleman all evening. Then clusters of mistletoe had suddenly appeared over all the couples, a magical feat that Lily still didn't quite grasp.

Still, she'd embraced the tradition and grinned up at him as she said, "Looks like we have no choice." She'd pushed up onto her tiptoes, more than ready to taste the gorgeous man she'd been trying not to lust over for several weeks.

But he'd stepped back, shook his head, and apologized. Then he was gone, leaving her alone on the dancefloor while couples all around her kissed their partners in celebration of the Christmas season.

It was the second time in a month that she'd put herself out there and been rejected. After those two rejections and the messy breakup with her ex a few years before, she'd decided that dating was just off the table. She had a son to raise, and she didn't need the hassle of trying to figure out anyone else's intentions. She had her friends and her son, and that was enough for her.

Or at least she'd thought it was until she saw Holly and Ilsa with their husbands. Both of them were blissfully happy, and although Lily was happy for them, it didn't change the fact that she felt an ache when she noticed the quiet moments between them. Or when Zach brought Mia to Love Potions nearly every day so that Ilsa could have breakfast with them on her break. What would it have been like to have a partner like that while she was raising Evan?

She let out a sigh and glanced out the window.

"What's going on in that head of yours?" Chase asked as he slowed to take a narrow curve on Hwy 50. They were on their way to South Lake Tahoe to pick up a fancy new espresso machine for Love Potions, where they both still worked. It was the busy season, and the one at the store had given out that morning, leaving them in a bind. Mrs. Pottson had found one, but they had to either pick it up or wait for delivery. Chase had offered, and when he'd asked Lily to come along to help him do some shopping for his nieces, she'd reluctantly agreed. Apparently, there was a custom doll shop in the city that both the girls had fallen in love with on a summer trip earlier that year, and Chase didn't really understand how it all worked.

Lily decided she must be a sucker for helping the men of Christmas Grove shop because she hadn't been able to say no. "Nothing," she said. "Just thinking about all the things I need to get done this holiday season. You know, decorating, collecting toys, shopping, making cookies for Evan's school."

"Want some help with the cookies?" he asked. "I might know someone who's pretty good in the kitchen." He winked at her.

"Oh? You mean like Holly?" she said, purposely acting as if she hadn't known he meant himself. The man was a chocolatier for goodness sake. Any cookie he made would rival Martha Stewart's.

He laughed. "Sure. Holly makes great Christmas cookies. But she can't match my holiday penguins."

That was the truth. He made black and white cookies that were in the shape of penguins with Santa hats and red bows around their necks, and they were so delicious they were sinful. "I'm not sure six- and seven-year-olds can really appreciate your genius just yet, but I'll consider your offer."

"Tough crowd," he said, but he smiled at her.

"Sorry." She didn't mean to be such a pain. It was just hard to keep her guard up when he kept flirting with her.

They were silent for a bit as he drove over the mountain, but when they neared an exit for a ski resort, he said, "I need to stop off for some gas."

She nodded. "Maybe we can get a coffee while we're here?"

"Sure thing." He whipped the SUV into a gas station, filled up, and then took her to a nearby mom-and-pop coffee shop.

She hopped out and laughed when she spotted Christmas elves peeping at them from behind the bushes. They were all wearing ridiculous outfits and holding signs that said things like: *Looking for work Dec 26th*, *Will work for cookies*, and *Skilled warehouse worker, but I'd prefer something on the beach.*

"You have a pretty laugh," Chase said.

She turned to look at him. "Are you flirting with me again, Chase?"

He shrugged one shoulder. "Maybe. Is that bad?"

Yes! She mimicked his shrug. "No. I guess not."

Smiling, he placed his hand on her lower back and led her up to the counter. They placed their orders and a few minutes later, they were sitting at a table with their drinks and pastries.

"I have a confession to make," he said after taking a sip of his coffee.

"What's that?" she asked, staring at him and hating that he was so beautiful. Her fingers itched to touch that stubble again, and she mentally admonished herself.

No.

Where was her willpower when it came to this man? She was not putting herself out there again. Her ego couldn't take it. Or maybe it was her heart that was too bruised. Either way, she had no business thinking about him that way.

"I regret pulling away from you when we were under the mistletoe last year at the Christmas Ball."

Lily blinked at him, certain she hadn't heard him correctly. "What?"

"I've regretted not kissing you for all these months." His gaze bored into hers, and there was no misunderstanding this time.

She cleared her throat. "Why?"

Chase chuckled. "That's a loaded question."

She frowned. "I don't think so." She put the cup down that she'd been holding with both hands. "Listen, Chase, I think it's no secret that I'm attracted to you." Goodness. Had she just said that out loud? Judging by the self-satisfied look on his face, she most certainly had. Clearing her throat, she added, "But I'm not really looking for anything serious. And because I have a son, I can't afford to do anything casual. So let's just be friends, all right?"

Not looking for anything serious? Had she lost her mind? That was the only thing she was looking for. But she wasn't going to tell him that.

He pressed his lips together, and an unidentifiable emotion flashed in his eyes. Was that disappointment or confusion that she saw? She wasn't sure.

"All right," he finally said, keeping whatever he was thinking close to the vest. "Friends it is. Can a friend ask another friend out to dinner every once in a while?"

"That sounds like a date," she said.

"Not if it doesn't end in kissing," he countered with a smile.

Lily rolled her eyes. "I guess friends can grab dinner. But only if they meet there and each pay their own way."

He laughed. "Okay. I'm glad we cleared that up. Dinner then? Friday at Mistletoe's?"

"Maybe," she said, both wary and excited. She liked him. Wanted to spend time with him outside of work. She just didn't know if she could be disciplined enough to keep her hands to herself if he tried to kiss her. "I need to check and see if Ilsa can take Evan. My son and her stepson have gotten close, and they spend a lot of time together."

"Sounds good. Let me know. If Friday doesn't work, we'll try for another evening."

When they were done with their pastries, they climbed back into the SUV. But when Chase put the key in the ignition and tried to start it, nothing happened. He tried again. Still nothing.

"Damn," he said, closing his eyes. "That isn't good."

Lily glanced at him. "Do you know what it is?"

He shook his head. "Could be a couple things. Ignition, starter, something electrical. Time to call a tow truck."

To Lily's surprise, it didn't take long to get the SUV towed to the small repair shop in the tiny town and have diagnostics run.

"It's the starter," the mechanic told Chase. "I can get it done for you by tomorrow afternoon."

"Tomorrow!" Lily said. "But I need to get home tonight. I have to pick up my son from the sitter and—"

"I'm sorry, ma'am," the mechanic said. "The part is in Sacramento. The earliest we can get it is tomorrow morning."

"Is there a place to rent a car around here?" Chase asked.

He shook his head. "No, but there's a hotel down the street."

"Thank you. I appreciate the help." Chase led Lily away from the shop and started walking toward the hotel.

"I have to get home to Evan," Lily said, panicking a little. They'd left early enough that if everything had gone according to plan, they'd be back in town by eight. Lily's dad was down with the flu, so she had to find a backup to watch her son. Her neighbor had been willing to watch Evan, but Millie was elderly, and an overnight stay would be hard on her.

"Can you call Ilsa? See if she can help?" he asked. "Or maybe one of your friends can come pick you up, and I can deal with the car and espresso machine tomorrow."

"Let me see what I can do," Lily said. While speaking to Ilsa, Lily learned that Holly and Rex and their baby Zoe were in Keating Hollow for a few days. Zach was busy at the Christmas tree farm, and Ilsa was stuck at home with Mia, who had an upset tummy. So getting someone to pick her up was out of the question, but Ilsa did offer to pick Evan up from Millie's and keep him overnight. That was a relief at least. After thanking Ilsa and promising to return the favor, she tucked her phone away and looked up at Chase. "Looks like I'm staying here in this little ski town."

"All right," he said, giving her a bright smile as he held his hand out to her. "Let's make the best of it then."

"Friends, remember?" she said even as she slipped her hand in his.

"Right. Friends who are going to have dinner tonight." He winked at her and tugged her down the street to the hotel.

When they arrived, Lily went to the small store in the lobby while Chase went to check in. She purchased some toiletries and a change of clothes for both of them. When Chase returned, he handed her some cash for his items and they headed up to their rooms.

Correction. *Room.*

As Chase opened the door, he said, "This is the last one they had available."

Lily's stomach did somersaults as she walked into the room and saw only one bed. She glanced at him and felt her face flush pink.

Holy Christmas. How in the world was she going to stay *just friends* with Chase Garland when she'd be alone with him for an entire night in a tiny ski town where no one else knew them and they had to share a bed?

"Think of it as an adventure," he said then pointed up.

Her eyes went wide as she spotted the mistletoe hanging in the small hallway.

"I think it might be fate," he said as he tugged her to him. "What do you say, Lily? Just this once for Christmas tradition?"

All of her willpower dissolved as she stared up at his handsome face. And then she kissed him.

DEANNA'S BOOK LIST

Witches of Keating Hollow:
Soul of the Witch
Heart of the Witch
Spirit of the Witch
Dreams of the Witch
Courage of the Witch
Love of the Witch
Power of the Witch
Essence of the Witch
Muse of the Witch
Vision of the Witch

Witches of Christmas Grove:
A Witch For Mr. Holiday
A Witch For Mr. Christmas
A Witch For Mr. Winter

Premonition Pointe Novels:

Witching For Grace
Witching For Hope
Witching For Joy
Witching For Clarity

Jade Calhoun Novels:
Haunted on Bourbon Street
Witches of Bourbon Street
Demons of Bourbon Street
Angels of Bourbon Street
Shadows of Bourbon Street
Incubus of Bourbon Street
Bewitched on Bourbon Street
Hexed on Bourbon Street
Dragons of Bourbon Street

Pyper Rayne Novels:
Spirits, Stilettos, and a Silver Bustier
Spirits, Rock Stars, and a Midnight Chocolate Bar
Spirits, Beignets, and a Bayou Biker Gang
Spirits, Diamonds, and a Drive-thru Daiquiri Stand
Spirits, Spells, and Wedding Bells

Ida May Chronicles:
Witched To Death
Witch, Please
Stop Your Witchin'

Crescent City Fae Novels:
Influential Magic
Irresistible Magic
Intoxicating Magic

Last Witch Standing:
Bewitched by Moonlight
Soulless at Sunset
Bloodlust By Midnight
Bitten At Daybreak

Witch Island Brides:
The Wolf's New Year Bride
The Vampire's Last Dance
The Warlock's Enchanted Kiss
The Shifter's First Bite

Destiny Novels:
Defining Destiny
Accepting Fate

Wolves of the Rising Sun:
Jace
Aiden
Luc
Craved
Silas
Darien
Wren

Black Bear Outlaws:
Cyrus
Chase
Cole

Bayou Springs Alien Mail Order Brides:
Zeke

Gunn
Echo

ABOUT THE AUTHOR

New York Times and USA Today bestselling author, Deanna Chase, is a native Californian, transplanted to the slower paced lifestyle of southeastern Louisiana. When she isn't writing, she is often goofing off with her husband in New Orleans or playing with her two shih tzu dogs. For more information and updates on newest releases visit her website at deannachase.com.

Made in the USA
Las Vegas, NV
14 March 2022

45590061R00142